Hank Emerson
1947-2023

The Pathfinder is dedicated to the memory of my life-long friend, Hank. I can still see us playing on the beach at Chesuncook Village, driving the boat up the West Branch to fish, and gamboling over, under and through the dri-ki as we went to greet the mail boat. I was faster than you on our Flexible Fliers, but you were always far ahead on the ski slopes, waiting for me to catch up. Rest well, my dear friend.

This is a work of fiction. Names, characters, businesses, places, events and incidents are either the product of the author's imagination or used in a fictitious manner. Any resemblance to actual persons, living or dead or actual events is purely coincidental.

Cover design and illustrations by Taylore Aussiker

Printed in the United States of America
First Printing, August 2023
ISBN 978-1-7339153-4-2
'Suncookers LLC, publisher

Suncookersworld.com

taussikerdesigns.com

The Pathfinder

Book three of the *'Suncookers* series

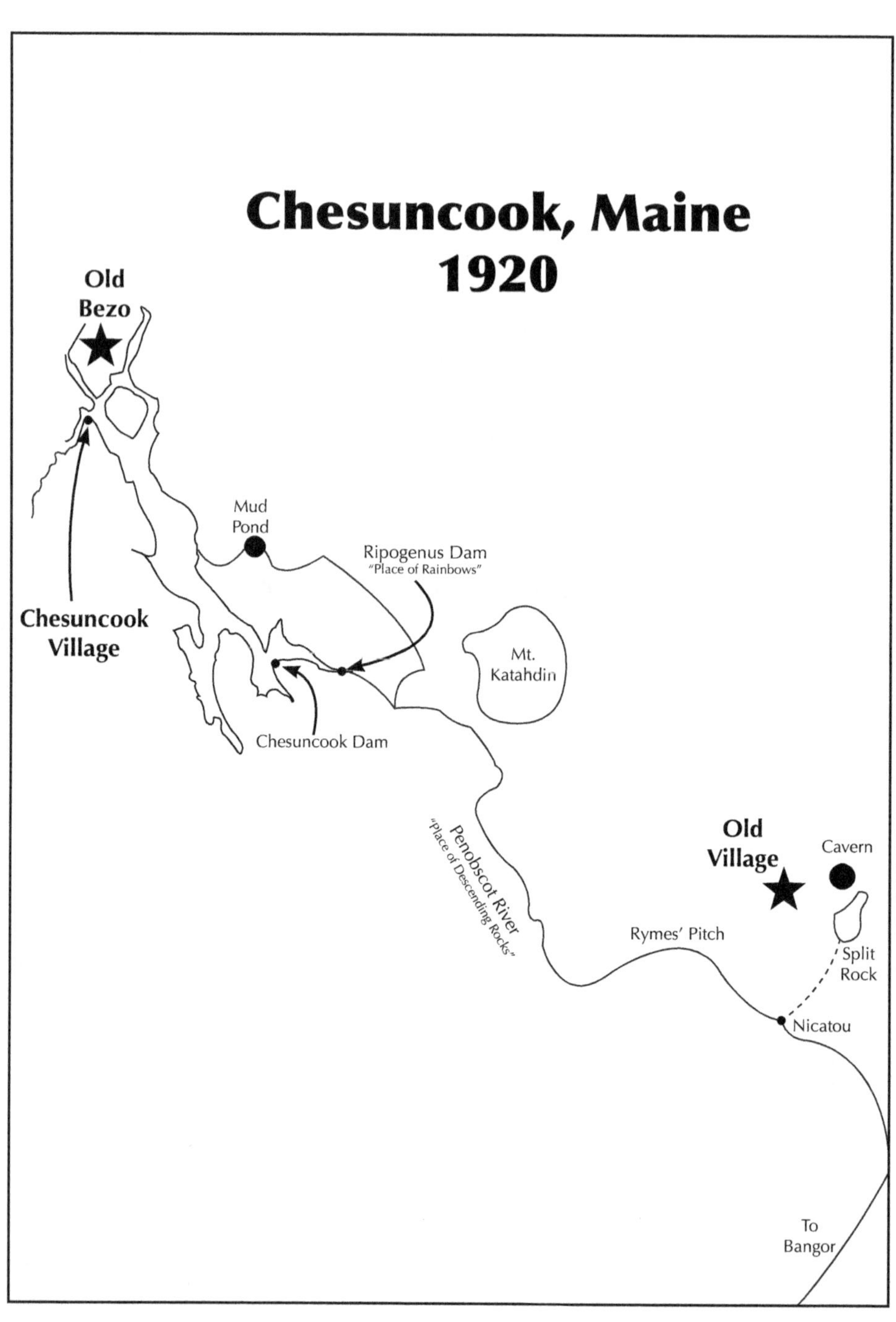

Chesuncook, Maine
1920
Old
Bezo
Chesuncook
Village
Mud
Pond
Ripogenus Dam
"Place of Rainbows"
Mt.
Katahdin
Chesuncook Dam
Penobscot River
"Place of Descending Rocks"
Old
Village
Cavern
Rymes' Pitch
Split
Rock
Nicatou
To
Bangor

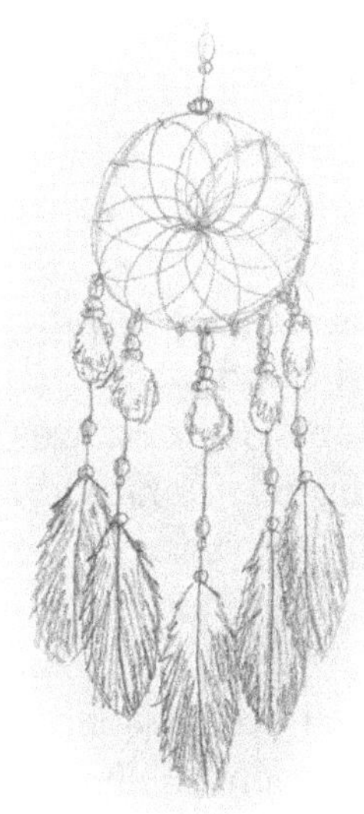

Back Home
Chapter 1

Ka-boom! With an instant clap of thunder, a flash of lightning split the sky, shooting out from a black cloud crossing just north of the Dam. This storm would miss, but the next one would swoop farther south and hit us. We were waiting for our ride home, having been away about a week visiting with Abby's Grandmother Molly.

"Watch her surf down those swells," I said. The north wind was pretty strong, blowing the foam straight off the peaking whitecaps. *The Twilight*'s bow cut into the giant waves like a plow going through the snow.

"It won't be much fun heading into that going home, Charlie," Abby said.

"Maybe we'll have to wait until it calms down." We'd done that many times before, sometimes motoring up in the dark after the wind backed off.

It was late spring of 1923. Abby and I were returning to our remote village, a crossroads for the Abenaki Nation then and immigrant loggers now. We were called "'Suncookers," residents of Chesuncook Village, a settlement that supported the cutting and transportation of logs for lumber and paper making. Our village now had seventy-five residents, half year-round and half seasonal workers on the log drives. We had our own church, school, store and post office. We were almost civilized. Bangor, the nearest big city some hundred miles away, was the destination of all the wood cut here. There was a hand-crank phone network that connected us and the logging camps with the central switchboard at the Grant Farm, some twenty miles away.

"It won't be calm until morning," Abby said. "When the clouds are this low, there won't be a break in the wind gusts for a while." She was right. The sky looked like it held a lot of wind in those black clouds and wouldn't die down until daybreak. Slate grey rollers came around the point, turning the float into a bucking bronco.

Making and running moonshine was the King's family business since the start of Prohibition in January of 1920. By the end of that year, our sales of *Tanglefoot* Whiskey made us a lot of money, but there was a cost. Mother had died in the hotel fire, and my new friend, Tommy died with her, trapped in the top floor by a fire our competition started. Three years later, we were still looking over our shoulders wondering when the Boston Gang would try again.

It wasn't only the bad boys from Boston that was a concern. Two years ago, I lived in a nightmare that I couldn't seem to shake. It wasn't just the detritus of a bad dream. I was followed by a creature with giant black wings, coal red eyes and razor sharp talons. The black wings never seemed to catch up with me, but lurked in the distance as if to let me know I could be easily found even across the centuries. The wings would follow us up the lake and at a distance, hunting just above the pointed firs along the shore.

We watched *The Twilight* make its way between the channel markers and aim for the dock. Abby and I walked out over the catwalk to the little float where she would tie up. Chained to the pier, the float was moved away from shore as the water continued to drop. The big pulp flush had ended a few days ago, but more water was going to be needed to flush it further downstream. The dock would have to be moved every few days now, or it would be left high and dry. We hoped the draw down would not force us to tie up at the end of the pier where there was little protection from the wind.

"I was hoping we would rest here a bit before we went back up the lake," I said.

"Because?"

"Because I want to be sure that things are just like we left them." She knew what I meant. We had become time travelers while helping Abby's Grandmother Molly fight an illness in her village, an illness that modern medicine could not help with. We brought back special plants she needed from Grey Wolf's village. Grey Wolf was Grandmother Molly's father. Thirty-five hundred years ago, he sent Grandmother Molly to our time for her protection.

Sometimes things didn't work out the way Abby planned. She

was the only one who held the amulet, knew the ritual and what words turned the clock one way or the other and by how much. There was a block of stone where the amulet had to be placed. My job was to be holding Abby's hand. Only then would I be able to travel with her. One time we walked out of the cavern to find a world frozen in ice. We never knew if we were in the right place until we walked out of the cave to see. We nearly froze to death crawling back inside so we could try again. If anything happened to the amulet, we'd be stuck back there, thirty-five hundred years ago for the rest of our lives. That would cause more than a few ripples in time.

"You don't think we're in the right timestream, do you?" she asked, grasping the amulet she wore under her shirt as if the pressure of her palm would give some assurance that all was well. This uncertainty was mostly my own anxiety coming to the surface.

"I don't know. I just worry about it. Remember how we thought we were gone from Nicatou for a couple of days, but it was really four or five in current time?"

"So, you think more than a week has passed since we left? You mean that time passes differently depending on where we are?"

"It seems to. Time seems to expand when we look at the future but it seems to compress when we look at the past. If things aren't adding up, we'll know soon. Here she comes."

The Twilight approached the float. Her exhaust gurgled louder as Uncle Amos threw her in reverse and revved up at the same time, acting as a brake. I ran for the stern line Louis threw out and had it snug around the dock's cleat while Abby pulled the bow snug against the float. *The Twilight* stopped moving. The little float strained away from the pier's support posts, chains holding it fast, as *The Twilight*'s forward motion was checked.

I could tell it was Uncle Amos at the helm the moment I saw the shadow of a briar pipe hanging from his mouth. He is my favorite uncle; heck, he's my only uncle! Amos was usually quiet, following Father's orders. My Uncle Amos was kind, understood how the family worked, and was a sounding board for all my worries. He was always neatly dressed, wool shirt, felt hat and a gold watch fob hanging from the black vest he always wore.

Louis tossed the stern line to me, and I snugged it up on a cleat. The float strained some more, chains rattling as the forward motion was checked. Father exploded out of the engine room, mug in hand, complaining about the government again. Father was a living bundle of determination. There was a lot of gear and a bunch of woodsmen coming out of camp now that the drive was nearly done. Louis was helping two men slide a stretcher over the gunwales. On the stretcher was a woodsman, his leg in a long splint, moaning at each rise and fall of the boat and over the dock.

"What happened to him?" I asked Louis as he balanced a crate on the gunwale. Louis came to the village as the telephone repair man, maintaining the single bare wire that connected all the cutting camps, depots and even the primitive homes in our village. The switchboard was at the Grant Farm, some twenty miles away. Sometimes, we could talk with Bangor or Boston if the wet branches on the line didn't short out the system too much. Not long after he arrived, we hired Louis to help us make and deliver *Tanglefoot* down the lake to a thirsty nation.

"Broken leg," Louis explained. "A log got him at the landing where they were rolling the wood into the river. He didn't jump out of the way in time. He's pretty lucky he didn't get squished into the sawdust or rolled into the current under the rest of the wood." I grabbed the rope handle at the other end of a crate and Abby and I slid it onto the dock. Then we dragged it over the gangplank and onto the shore. Soon, there were five more crates the same size stacked up by the shoreline, waiting to be loaded into a truck. "Produit du Canada" was stamped on the ends, and "Thompson .45" under it. A delivery for the Boston gang, I guessed. I found a canvas to cover them so no one would see what we were shipping. I didn't feel good about this part of Father's business. Someday there would be payback for being a back woods arms dealer. I could feel it.

It was too rough to take the boat back to the Village, so we stayed that night. Abby and I bunked in the hayloft in the barn as lightning continued to dance around us until dawn. We were safe from drunks at least because they wouldn't be able to make it up the ladder to the loft where we had made our nest for the night. Our only concern was a barn fire from a lightning strike.

We were up at dawn the next morning to see a beautiful blue-sky day, ate right after the river drivers got out of the dining room, then loaded the supplies that were piled on our two trucks we kept in the barn. We made countless trips back over the gangplank, over the bobbing, wet float, transferring the load to *The Twilight*. At times it was like walking a tightrope while carrying a glass of water. Possible, but not easy.

A dozen men and their gear were waiting to load. Mostly

immigrants, they were "picking the rear." They walked the sides of the river, pulling logs that had stuck along the shore back into the current. They loaded their own gear as Louis, Abby and I arranged it in one long pile along the centerline of the rear deck.

"Don't forget to make room for those crates of empty bottles," Father yelled to us as he came over the gunnel, spilling coffee as he swung his leg to the deck. "And we need to fuel up, too." He disappeared into the little cabin and shut the door. It was probably time to add a squirt of special *Tanglefoot* blend to his coffee mug.

The Twilight's engine caught right away, and after she warmed up, Louis untied the bow line, jumping on with the rope in his hand, and I did the same with the stern line. Uncle Amos backed her away from the pier in no time. He swung the bow sharply and gave it full throttle as we yawed our way into the channel. The sudden change in motion made staying upright a challenge. Father stayed in the closed-up cabin, drinking his pale colored "coffee" and probably imagining a new scheme to make him rich. The river drivers were sitting on side benches and piles of freight, busy with briar pipes and hand-rolled cigarettes.

I wanted to talk with Uncle Amos, but not with Father in ear shot. I wanted to know more about the new business. I decided to start with Louis, and I moved toward him as he was relaxing in the bright sun on the upholstered stern seat, the American flag on a short staff flying behind him, *The Twilight*'s gurgling wisps of exhaust fading behind.

"Tell me some more about the new business arrangements," I asked, sitting beside him and pointing to a teetering pile of crates. "Where do those come in?"

Louis looked at the pile of empty crates from the last delivery, and turned to me. "Caleb made a deal with the Boston gang. We occasionally smuggle arms from Quebec to Bangor. From there, a schooner takes them the rest of the way to Boston. He's paid well. We're making a lot of money on the booze, too. There are some big orders ahead. The guns are something Caleb had no choice about."

"But it's not just guns, is it?" I asked.

"No. Some pretty hot guys need cooling off in Canada, so we smuggle them in when we drop off the guns. It's pretty easy, but I wonder if it's a one-way trip for them, know what I mean?" Louis looked up at me from the railing. "Some of them are pretty jumpy."

"You mean they might just disappear for good after they walk into the woods?"

"Something like that, I guess." Louis grimaced. "For some, I think they use cement overshoes in Boston Harbor, maybe. All depends on how much of a threat they are."

I also wanted to get an idea of how much money we're sharing in the "family" business, but Louis might not know those important details. I wanted to keep him out of that discussion as long as I could. He's a worker-bee, and although a good friend, Louis is not a member of our family, so I decided to ask Amos directly. Father would blow a gasket if I asked him. He'd turn red, swallow and choke on the poor excuse of a cigar racing around his mouth at probably anything I asked, so usually I kept quiet around him. I kept thinking of grabbing Abby and putting the miles away every time the business got more dangerous. I can say I'd rather not have to roll logs off the river bank or pick a jam the rest of my life, and running rum was just as risky. But smuggling people? That was easier to pull off than disguising cases of moonshine in a box labeled "Bibles." The Sheriff and deputies wouldn't bother about an extra person or two, dressed up like Russian immigrant wood cutters, white fingers grabbing hold of the benches in the back of the truck as we rumbled over the rough, washed-out dirt roads.

Little Mouser Island slid behind us. I walked to the bow lost in thought about money and black wings when I felt Abby's arms come around me. She rested her cheek against my back and squeezed me hard while *The Twilight* made her way around Weymouth Point. We were now heading in back of Gero Island for the Thoroughfare to the Cuxabexis Depot. Delivering supplies for the Company was part of our business, but making and smuggling *Tanglefoot* is what made the money.

"I worry about what's in those crates," I said. We were standing on the bow of the boat, leaning against the chain railing. The morning's ride was crisp, a cold front coming through, kicking up some good white caps. We were so heavy that we just cut through it all, glassy water peeling away from the bow. Clouds were getting lower, and the wind was fixing to change direction. Weather was coming in, and we'd be wet before we got home.

"It's a dangerous business," Abby pointed out. We came closer to the center of the Thoroughfare. I sensed something behind us and turned to see. Ducking in and out of the shadows around the tops of the fir and spruce trees, black wings and coal red eyes were keeping a close watch.

"I wonder about the nest, too," I sighed. "I can't stop thinking about it."

"Can't you leave it be?" There was a frown on her face.

"'Fraid not," I smiled. "Especially when the black wings are still keeping an eye on me. Sometimes thoughts stick around for a reason." The smile left my face. "Something's been left undone. I can feel it."

"We don't know what happened after we left, but we can do only so much without upsetting our present, like families disappearing." She was right. It had happened before when we brought back Little Rabbit. She had to go back. The Mitchell family, her descendants, lived in Grandmother Molly's village where we had been visiting. But they disappeared without a trace as if a magician had waved his magic wand just as soon as we brought Little Rabbit back to our time. She didn't belong. When the timestream is changed, most anything can happen. And we see only the obvious difference right away.

"There were eggs ready to hatch," I pointed out.

"But the Nighthawk fell out of the aerie in the form of Blackfeather. I thought it was all over." I was knocked off the ledge at the same time, but caught a branch and was able to pull myself up.

"When I was climbing back into the cave, I looked over my shoulder and saw Blackfeather turn into Ki'kwa'jenu just before hitting the boulders below. It buzzed off into the night."

Ki'kwa'jenu, the Abenaki name for nighthawk, was my nemesis. It had the power to appear like a person, and it did so by taking the form of a hunter named Blackfeather. Blackfeather was a force of evil. I had something it wanted, and that had to do with a certain ability I developed: I could summon the South Wind Sowanakik when I was really angry. Sometimes trees would uproot before Abby could calm me down. I thought the power over Sowanakik was what Ki'kwa'jenu wanted. I could often see the nighthawk's coal-red eyes burning in my direction all the way from Caucmagomic Ridge, far across the lake, watching. Other times, its black wings would be following me in the distance, waiting. I battled Blackfeather in the nighthawk's aerie, but in the end, it escaped.

"That means….," Abby paused.

"That means Ki'kwa'jenu is probably alive and well, feeding on what it has captured." I looked behind us. Abby let go and pulled her cloak tightly around herself. "That would explain the black wings chasing us up the lake, hiding in the tree tops. They're bigger, and it's bolder coming out during the day. It must be stronger somehow. I worry about Grey Wolf's people."

On our last visit, we pulled Little Rabbit from the Nighthawk's aerie, and doing so had not seemed to upset our present. But when we brought her home to out time, an entire familial line in Grandmother Molly's present village disappeared, farm buildings and relatives never having existed.

We could see the top of the cliffs as we entered the Thoroughfare.

"I want to know what's left in the aerie," I said. "Come with me?"

"Someone needs to keep track of you, in case," Abby said with a smile and took my hand. The clear skies had given way to a line of drizzle-like showers. Mist had closed down over the top of the cliff. We could see almost to the tops of the pines but nothing more.

"In case?" I asked.

"Just in case," she replied. We left the consequences of the trip hanging in the air like the descending mist around the aerie.

The rain held off while we unloaded the Depot's order at the Cuxabexis dock. The rivermen being delivered to the camp did the toting to the cookhouse/dining room. All we had to do was to slide the cargo from the boat to the dock. The hardest were the barrels of potatoes, crates of onions, and the molasses that had to be rolled up a plank over the gunwales. With our own human chain of river drivers, the supplies were safely off the boat and in the storehouse when we cast off.

The water this time of year was lower than expected; not enough snow melt, not enough fall or spring rains. We were going to be lucky if there was enough to float our winter's work down Caucmagomic Stream after the company got their wood flushed downriver. There was a different feeling with the wind blowing out of Umbazookus instead of out of the West Branch. It was a cold October wind, not a warm May one, as it should have been. Usually, it would be September before we noticed the scent of wet mud flats drying in the hot sun over Goose Grass Flats, not May. Steady waves kept their shapes, sharp angles coming to ever increasing peaks of foam while the temperature plummeted along the advancing cold front. Amos had to be careful with the old stumps that were poking through the surface, especially if he had been spiking his morning coffee like Father did. We were chugging through the middle of the channel when I thought I heard Abby gasp. I turned around to see her holding onto the chain rail, her other hand on the back of her head. Our sunny morning was no more. Misty clouds continued to drop. We'd be in the fog soon.

"Abby?" I asked, coming closer to her. "Are you okay? What's up?"

"Yeah, I just had the weirdest feeling. Isn't that where *The*

Tethys went down?" she said quietly so Father wouldn't hear us over the chugging of the engine. He hated to be reminded of that day when so many died.

"Just about a hundred feet in back of us," I replied. "I thought you knew where."

"Not until now," she said. "It's weird, like I could hear them screaming as they burned. I'll be really glad to get home." She was shivering, and I put my arms around her. I felt the only thing I could do was to hold her as if that alone was enough to keep her safe.

We could see our Katahdin View Inn just ahead. We came to the dock in the lee of the cove and tucked into the south side of the point where there was still deep water.

"Be sure you check the dock chains after you tie up. And use double lines!" Father shouted over his shoulder as he scurried up the gangplank. He probably thought he had to remind us to breathe and eat, too. I gave the chains a good shake, and all was in order. The duffel bags were so heavy that we had to drag them up the cement steps, making a right turn to the end of Olive Street, where our inn stood. We had to do laundry, put things away, and get ready for the next thing, whatever that would be.

Olive was working in the kitchen. "Hey, good to see you back," she said over a baked ham she was just sliding out from the oven.

"It's great to be back," Abby said. "Where's Anna? I thought she'd be helping out." Anna was Louis' young wife. Heck, they were both young, not much older than me or Abby. Anna had been recruited as a bar-girl in a Bangor speak-easy, and it was her good luck that Louis was her very first customer. They fell in love that night, and Louis broke her out of the worst place a young woman could be. They got married, and he brought her back to live in our little village. Their first child came right away.

"She's upstairs doing rooms," Olive said. "So I said I would watch the baby, and so far...." The baby started to cry. "....so far it's been okay." She threw a trivet onto the long counter and set down the pan. Then she turned to the potatoes on the stove.

"Many guests?" Abby asked as she walked over and picked up little Anna who was now screeching in the crib. The minute Abby picked her up, the infant quieted down.

"Full house just cleared out except for some Company men wanting lunch." She finished with a pan and set it aside. "There, the potatoes are done." Olive wiped her hands and reached for a serving dish. Abby quietly put the baby down and grabbed a serving spoon. I dropped my bags and headed for the sink to wash up.

"How are you doing with the old language?" she asked.

Olive was my step-mother. She had a round face, high cheekbones, dark hair and eyes to go with her dark brown skin. Olive was a member of the Wabanaki, People of the Dawnland. The most eastern people, Wabanaki were the first in the nation to see the dawn. Olive was our Abenaki language teacher, constantly drilling us on word meanings and pronunciations. Abby was pretty fluent, and my skills had improved a lot over the winter.

I answered in Abenaki.

"That sounds great. The biscuits are done. And they need to come out now!" Olive said fast as lightening, she flung open the oven door with her free hand. When the crisis passed, she shouted out a word, and Abby and I would compete to define it. Dinner got served, and the kitchen got cleaned up. Abby and I sat down for our own meal once the tray of cake went out to the dining room to satisfy the lodgers' sweet tooth. Anna was talking with some of the guests. It wasn't long before we collected the dessert plates, cleaned off the tables, being sure there was adequate sugar, salt, napkins and silverware for the morning's meal. The men would be hungry as they got ready for a long day's work up river. The last of the logs were coming through, and the men were picking the rear, getting stubborn pulp logs out of inlets, coves and the like. We still had our own logs to float down the stream from the landing above Black Pond. If they didn't get flushed down to the lake pretty soon, they'd be left high and dry until next spring. By then, they wouldn't be much good with the bugs chewing at them.

Anna and the baby left for their camp, while Abby and I unpacked. I started to dump the contents of my duffle on my bed when I happened to look out the window. I froze. There on the darkening ridge between Caucmagomic and Longley Stream were two ember-red dots that bored right into me. The clouds had disappeared once more, and the moon's pale light over Caucmagomic Mountain flowed like a river around my bed and the contents of my duffle. Tall spruce on the black ridge top were outlined as if drawn in black ink. And there they were, two glowing red dots. As their intensity waxed and waned, I wondered when I'd be seeing them closer.

Ki'kwa'jenu was back. I had a feeling that this time the Nighthawk would not go away easily.

Another Delivery
Chapter 2

One morning, a few days after we returned from visiting Grandmother Molly, I heard, "Charlie, come here!" as I trod down the stairs for breakfast. I was hoping to snag one of the muffins I had been smelling the past half hour. Now Father wanted me. Hopefully, after muffin time. I'd been giving my driving boots a good coat of bear grease to keep them waterproof. After I wiped the stinky stuff off my hands, I tied the laces together and slung them over my shoulder.

"I'm coming," I said. When I rounded the bottom landing into the great sitting room, Father was standing at the kitchen door, between me and muffins. My stomach growled with urgency.

"What'd you say?" Father asked.

"Nothing, it's my stomach growling. I haven't eaten since –"

"Okay, get something to eat." I could tell he was more impatient than usual. "Pack something for overnight. You're heading to the Dam by four. Load at least four barrels first, then back fill with cases, got it?" I nodded.

"When you get to the Dam, you'll get the trucks ready to make a delivery. You'll need to take Abby with you." He turned and headed outside.

Father's suggestions were nothing like 'think about it.' They were more like 'do this,' 'do that.' I didn't think I should be asking Abby. We could get stopped or worse. But I had my orders.

"I'll let her know," I said to his back and turned to find her. When I walked through the parlor, I saw her standing on the last landing, tying her fire-red hair behind her head.

"What's going on?" she asked. The pair of freshly greased boots I had brought downstairs were still draped over my shoulder.

"Not sure, but we have to make a delivery. Tonight. Father wants us to ride together, you know, extra eyes, just in case." At least we'd enjoy the ride out, driving the truck to market. We always had fun on the trip, and we always flipped a coin to see who got to drive first.

"When are we loading? I thought things were quieting down," Abby said as I walked through the kitchen, holding a newspaper under my newly greased boots so they wouldn't lubricate the kitchen floor.

"Right after I eat something, we start loading the boat. There are some big orders to fill. We shove off by four."

When we had returned from our first visit with Grandmother Molly, Abby was added to the King Moonshine Company's payroll, although she hadn't seen much money. Neither had I. We worked together every day with Uncle Amos running the stills and filling bottles, moving barrels and cases. Abby could run *The Twilight* after Uncle Amos showed her only once. She could drive the oxen, a team of horses, and could handle our modified Model-T trucks. Our trucks were top of the line with much more power once Amos had finished his modifications to the engines.

"I've seen them again," I said to Abby as I paused just beyond the lodge's staircase. The natural cedar posts on each side of the stairs were getting darker every year as the shellac that covered them aged and cracked in the sunlight.

"Where?" she asked, coming to a dead stop on the landing as I turned my head.

"There were red eyes on the ridge last night as I was unpacking," I said, and began thinking more about my breakfast.

"How long did they stay?"

"About a half hour," I replied. The sightings were becoming more frequent, and the eyes were staying visible longer each time. On our trip home, I saw the black wings way in the distance, rising and falling over the hills as we made our way up the lake. Then again that night. Not good. I followed Abby into the kitchen.

"The wind's coming up," Abby said, looking out the window over the sink as she filled the tea kettle.

"Full moon tonight, too," I added. Whenever there was a full moon, it got a lot colder for a night or two.

"The moonlight will help for the trip, right? We won't need the truck's lights?"

"Depends on how many clouds pass over. I hope we're not going down the Devil's Staircase. It's not something I want to drive without lights."

"Why, scared of ghosts?" Abby teased with that smile that melted my heart each time I saw it.

"Yeah, but just the spirits who push boulders off the cliff into the roadway."

"Oh," she said. "Those," she stopped smiling. We'd had a narrow scrape with a falling rock the last time we went that way. The giant boulder was right there in the middle of the second turn of Devil's Staircase, heading away from Sias Hill. Being the middle of the day, it was easy enough to see and get around it, our brakes were good, but had it been dark? We'd be a crumpled wreck at the bottom of the gorge, folks still figuring out how to winch out the remains. Just as I was buttering my first muffin, Uncle Amos walked in.

"Hey, Charlie, you two ready to get to work? We've got a lot of 'shine to load up." Uncle Amos folded his beret into his back pocket and reached for the coffee pot. He poured himself a mug and refilled mine. Abby brought our scrambled eggs over, and we ate our breakfast as Amos scribbled in the little notebook he always carried with him.

"We've already had our marching orders. What's that you were writing?" I asked.

"Inventory, mostly," he said. "Have to figure what supplies we need for the next few batches. They'll be coming back with us after the drop off."

"Supplies for more than one batch?" I asked. We never got more stuff than we needed, crafting just one batch of *Tanglefoot* at a time. Uncle Amos seemed to think of something, put down his mug and drew out his notebook again.

"Apparently Caleb got some new business, and we're going to have to work a little harder to fill all the orders," Amos explained. "Booze goes wherever there's a thirst for it!" he said as he did some more figuring with a stub of a pencil. He tore out a page.

"There are a few supplies to bring back," he said, putting away his little book again, pencil stub behind his ear. "Here's the list." Uncle Amos handed me a slip of paper. "Just take it from the storehouse at the Dam. Okay?"

"Why don't you come with us tonight?" I asked.

"I was planning to set up another batch while you were gone," he explained. The last time this happened, Father ran off on an errand

and Abby and I headed down river to her Grandmother Molly's, leaving Amos alone to do most of the work. I got that. There were many times the loading had to be done and I was the only one to do it. Twice as hard, twice as sore the next day.

"Nobody gives two eggs from the same hen!" Father roared as he flew through the doorway. "If you got a job to do, do it. Any breakfast left, Abby?" He sat down at his place beside me, hanging his hat on one of the posts of the ladder-chair's back.

"You can have this," she said as she slid her plate right in front of me. I slid it on to Father. She got up and put more eggs in the pan for us.

"We've got a tight time schedule," Father said, shoveling breakfast into his maw while reaching for a muffin at the same time. "Got any coffee?" he asked. "We have to be loaded to head down the lake by four. Then there's the transfer to the trucks, and you're off an hour later."

"Who's the customer?" I asked. Abby was pouring his coffee.

"Martin again," he said. And there's a new development," Father said. "I just learned that it's legal for a doctor to prescribe alcohol. There's a new business down river that's going to repackage our *Tanglefoot* to fill those prescriptions. And it's for sale, too!"

"We can afford to buy it?" I asked.

"Mostly," Father said with a smile. "The best part is that our government is helping us buy it." Apparently, the government that prohibited the sale of alcohol was helping us make alcohol for sale.

Abby set the coffee pot on a cast iron trivet on the table before returning to scramble eggs in the fry pan. Amos poured himself another cup.

"The delivery will take two trucks," Father replied. "Take the turn off to the Devil's Staircase so you can get to town the quickest way. I want you there at midnight. Do not leave the Dam before dark." The room was silent. Abby had stopped scrambling the eggs in the iron pan. Amos stopped dumping out Prince Albert curly-cut mid bowl as he took all this in.

"You're sending them down that road?"

"No choice, Amos," Father said, "and you're going to be driving the second truck with Louis." He didn't even look up from his plate. "You have to meet Martin's private train at the mill siding in Greenville by midnight. Sias Hill will take too long, and you're more likely to blow a tire on those sharp rocks." Eggs were scrambling again after Abby shot me a dark look. I tried to be disinterested.

"There's a lot riding on this delivery being on time," Father warned. He'd finished bolting his breakfast and gulping down the cup of hot coffee. This wasn't going to hurt my pocket. Or Abby's. It had been quite a while since we had been paid. "Get going as soon as you can," he instructed, grabbing his hat on the way out the door, his smokeless .41 holstered on his hip. "And tell Louis when you see him. He'll be riding with Amos."

The Devil's Staircase snaked over a mile of steep switchbacks. The tricky part began with a gradual downhill that belied what was to come, then suddenly snaked down the side of a mountain, high, sheer ledges on the mountain side. There wasn't much at all on the other side of that goat path but plenty of space to fly through the air if you didn't make the turn. And if you did make it, then maybe a boulder had tumbled down the mountain for a visit with its cousins in the middle of the road where you couldn't see it until it was too late.

We had two ways of getting there when we reached Lily Bay, if we reached Lily Bay. We could take the barge over Moosehead or wrestle with the new road up Sandy Bay Hill. It had been dry enough this May, so we could easily take the new road, cutting off more time.

"Let's get going," I said, standing up. Abby had finished her eggs.

"Not so fast, you." Abby said. "Come help with the dishes." I dried and we were done in moments.

"We need to pack some food," Abby said. "How long?"

"We'll be gone and back to the Dam before sunrise. Most of the driving will be in the dark," I said.

"So, some supper and something for an early breakfast on the road? And what about the guests?"

"Sounds good. I'll dig out the gear we'll need, then I'll go find Anna," I replied and finished lacing up my shoes. Olive needed her to help out whenever Abby and I made a delivery like this.

"Are you anxious about the Devil's Staircase?" Abby asked.

"I have to say that I am," I replied. "This is one time I wouldn't want to lose the coin toss to see who drives first."

"Why? Don't you trust my driving?"

"Of course, I trust your driving," I said with a bit of a snap. "But you know how anxious I can get sitting there helplessly while you wrestle with the wheel."

"Okay, calm down there, big boy. Maybe you'll win the toss after all, but I will be driving the truck if you lose, no matter how anxious you claim to be!" She stared at me a moment, her hands quietly on her hips. I tried not to laugh, but had I? Big trouble there.

The South Wind, Sowanakik, howled with a fierceness that uprooted trees whenever I got anxious or angry. This wasn't something I could always control. Once, after Mother and Tommy died in the hotel fire, I brought up such a wind that drowned the two men as they paddled away from their arson to what they believed was safety. There was no way they could survive in three-foot waves and a 50-mph south wind. More than a few trees came down that time. It had taken Abby ten minutes to get me to relax before the wind settled down. Mister Smith and Mister Wesson did not survive their canoe ride. Now, whenever the wind comes up from the south, folks around me turn and stare to see if maybe I might be the cause. If they saw that my eyeballs disappeared under my upper lids and I began to shake, they'd run to find Abby as she was the only person who could calm me down enough to keep trees from uprooting.

Abby packed up something to eat while Uncle Amos and I loaded the wagon for its first trip to *The Twilight*, now resting at the dock. Abby joined us before the first row of cases were slid onto the flat wagon. We put the side gates on before the horses hauled the buckboard to the dock. The cases all fit on the boat. *The Twilight* was sitting low in the water when we were done.

I had a pack basket with a change of clothes and a sleeping bag. Abby had the same, and we loaded those under the dry cabin roof. It was just in case, and I hoped we'd be back at the Dam by dawn tomorrow. I could feel a change in weather creeping closer. We had a north wind now, but it might be out of the south on the return trip. Getting pushed along was easier than pounding at each foamy crest.

While we were doing all the work, Father had taken his new steel boat up the river for some business he hadn't discussed. Uncle Amos, Abby and I were wary of his plans, but we felt locked into this family, crazy as Father was. We got our gear together and walked the pebble path to the boat. Louis was already there, pumping out the bilge. After we loaded the last of the Moxie that wasn't Moxie, Father returned from his business meeting and we were ready to head to the Dam.

Louis threw off the bow line and hopped aboard while I did the same with the stern. As Father backed out of the cove, I reminded myself about where the life jackets were if we went down. The stern was sitting pretty low, and a sudden stop might cause our own backwash to do just that, wash over our stern. The lake remained calm the entire trip and we tied up just before four P.M.

"Tell me again why it's called 'the Devil's Staircase?'" Abby asked. We were sitting on the bow, our legs dangling off the side, the cable of the railing taught against our chests as we stared at the parting waters of the lake.

"It's the switchbacks and the spirits," I said.

"I remember some of that now."

"Folks traveling that route often tell about someone sitting on a flat ledge that overlooks the road. Then, there's the ghost."

"Who is it? The same spirit?" Abby asked.

"No, they're different descriptions. Some see a woman, others a man. The image doesn't last long. No one knows why they appear."

Mt. Katahdin was brilliant in the sun, a little snow still dressing the peak. It was a lot colder a mile up there. When it rained in the Village this time of year, it snowed on the mountain.

Father was in the boat's cabin taking a nap. Uncle Amos throttled back as we approached the pier. *The Twilight* slid beside the float. Abby hopped out the stern and caught the rear cleat with that rope while I threw the bow rope onto the dock so she could snag the front cleat. Running over slippery logs seemed no challenge to her, just like the time she scampered up and down a log jam to help an injured river driver caught on top of the pile that was starting to haul. She was like a cat, never missing a step no matter how slippery the logs.

Uncle Amos shut the engine down, and we secured all the lines. Father roared back to life, popped out of the cabin and hurried to the Boom House to see the cook with a personal delivery of a bottle of our best. We walked up to the large barn to the trucks. There were two Model-T trucks, slightly modified for rum running. Each had an extra wide flat bed with canvas over hoops for a rear cover. The rigs looked like Conestoga wagons. Stitched together with heavy twine at the front, the canvas kept the rain out, but wasn't so good keeping out the clouds of road dust that sifted in through everything. Sometimes, cases and barrels had to be hosed off at delivery or the buyers threatened to hold back some cash. An opening covered with a trap door was cut into the floor boards right over the muffler. It was easily reached from the shotgun seat. If we were chased by revenooers, then the door was opened and used motor oil was poured onto the hot muffler. The smoke screen developing behind the truck would last for a mile or two while we made our escape down a side road. Our engines had more horsepower than most other vehicles on the road, except other runners maybe. Uncle Amos had redesigned the fuel system to give more gas, and more power. And then there was the nail defense. Nails were packed in two boxes bolted to the rear bumper. Two cables went from the catch on the box to the cab. If the cable was pulled, the box would open and long, sharp slivers of steel would spread all over the road behind. The hope was that the pursuing tires would puncture and we'd get away.

"This one's been moved," Uncle Amos observed after we rolled back the giant wooden doors that hung from pulleys rolling over an iron track.

"How do you know?" Abby asked.

"Tire tracks are fresher here," pointing out the fresh grooves in the soft dirt.

"I thought Father had some guy come to work on them," I said.

"Yeah, I do recall him talking about that last week," Uncle Amos said. "We'd best get these two down to the float. Abby, you drive this one down while Charlie sees if he can find some muscle to help. Okay, Charlie? Just check with the Cookee and see if there might be any stragglers that missed their wake-up call to go play on the river. I'll move the other truck."

"You got it," I said and began the walk to the Boom House. Maybe there'd be a donut in it for me.

"And Charlie?" Uncle Amos yelled. I stopped and turned. "See if you can bring down some donuts for all of us, okay?"

"Right," I said, and kept on my way.

It wasn't long before I brought back a plate of sugared donuts. We snacked and then went to work, lifting crates to the dock from *The Twilight*, and then bringing these up the gangplank to the waiting trucks. Two guys showed up looking for a bottle, the promised payment. After that, the crates practically flew off the boat. Barrels took the most time. They rolled easily, but it was tough to muscle them up the gangplank. Getting them up the second ramp to the truck bed was a different challenge. We had rigged up a rope and pulley system and winched up the barrels.

"That's the last one," I heard Uncle Amos say. "Charlie? Come help with the bilge."

That was the worst job. There were two bilge pumps, one at each side. My guess was that the heavy load had loosened up some planks and we'd have a lot to pump out. But *The Twilight* was well made, and we weren't five minutes at it until we came up dry.

"Let's double check the lines and see if we can add bumpers," Uncle Amos said. Abby slid the bumpers over the side and we tightened the lines so they'd stay between the boat and the dock. Father stopped by to check on our work.

"I'm heading down river to meet a guy," he said. "I'll take one of the horses and will be back around first light." Once his announcement was made, he turned on his heel and marched up to the big barn to confer with the stable hand and select a horse.

We finished loading by sunset. It was a quick fuel, oil and water check, and we were off in the dust. I lost the coin toss, so Abby was driving our truck. Uncle Amos followed with Louis riding shotgun. We put the dusty miles behind us, the trucks swaying with the heavy loads. Beavers had been busy, and now water was flowing over the roadway here and there. The dirt road was solid, even the bottoms of mud puddles were firm. We rolled slowly through those tiny lakes just the same.

After the Grant Farm, we came to a fork in the road where one way went up Sias Hill and the other dove down the side of the mountain, circling to a different direction along the hill's shoulder. We stopped a minute to let Uncle Amos and Louis catch up.

"There's the turn to the Devil's Staircase," I said. "Kill the lights in case someone's waiting for us." The moon was bright enough, a giant flashlight releasing the woods from their usual darkness.

"I can't wait," said Abby, flipping off the light switch while her hands tightened around the steering wheel. We were starting the descent to the first sharp turn. I could see her knuckles were already turning white. I know mine were, gripping the sides of my seat cushion.

The Devil's Staircase
Chapter 3

"Shouldn't we be slowing down?" I asked as we picked up speed.

"I'm trying to," Abby shouted over the whine of the transmission. She had been driving since the turn off before Sias Hill. "But we've lost our brakes!" Every second that passed found us rolling a little faster and now the first curve was coming up.

"Emergency brake?" I asked, moving my hands from the seat cushion to the panic bar I had bolted to the dashboard, my eyes getting wider as the road sloped away ahead of us. Overloaded did not begin to describe what we were carrying down the Devil's Staircase. Uncle Amos and Louis were behind us, reflections of the full moon occasionally glinting off their polished chrome front bumper in the rear-view mirror.

"It doesn't seem to be connected to anything," she shouted. "They worked fine until we went through that puddle." We were picking up speed and fast closing in on the first turn to the right. We might make that one, but the second one was much sharper, and the drop off was, well, stunning from a tourist's point of view. "You try it!" she shouted over the complaining whine of the truck. I reached over for the brake lever and gave it a yank.

"Nope, no good!" I reported, having hoped for a different result. The lever flopped down, seemingly disconnected from anything. Things were getting pretty bumpy with the heavy load in back leaning the truck one way and then the other. I thought we were going to roll it.

"We won't make the second turn," Abby shouted again.

"We don't have to. There's a logging trace that goes straight ahead up a little rise," I explained. Traces were just that. A trace of a winter road that was passable only with packed snow filling in the low spots. Usually these were free from obstructions like fallen logs. Little evidence of their existence remained once the snow had melted.

"That's right, I remember seeing it, but aren't there stumps? Help me with the wheel. It's getting harder to hold on to." I reached over to help pull the leaning truck into the travel lane. The wheels settled down, and now all four were on the ground.

"Maybe no stumps, unless they're hiding under the ferns! Can't you get it into a lower gear?"

"I don't dare. If I blow the shift, we'll have no engine brake. Third is better than neutral."

The second turn was coming up fast. The engine was screaming.

"There's the second turn!" I shouted. "I don't see any stumps in the run-out."

"Hold on!" Abby yelled. The gearbox whining, the engine clattering, the entire truck groaning from its cargo, we shot off the road, landing in marsh grass up to the hubs after a few big bounces. We were thrown against the windshield, but the glass didn't break and we were only bruised a little. If I search enough, I can still feel the resulting lump on my head.

I looked over at Abby, her knuckles white against the black rim of the steering wheel. "You can let go now," I suggested. "Nice driving, by the way."

"My fingers feel glued to the steering wheel." She relaxed her fingers, first one hand and then the other. Abby stepped out. I had to crawl out her side as my door was too close to a spruce tree to open enough.

"Hey! Look up there!" Abby pointed to a rock shelf above the sharpest part of the turn. I just had my head out of the cab and looked to where she was pointing. Someone was standing there. A wide, black band was painted across his eyes and temples. There were fine, long white stripes, like tears, drawn down each side of his face from his eyes to his lower jaw line. One hand held a spear, a string of feathers flying down its side in the night breeze. The spear point was brilliant in the moonlight. Slung over his back was an unstrung bow and a quiver of arrows. The warrior beckoned us with his free hand. Come, he seemed to say.

"If I didn't know any better, I'd say that was Moosis," I said. And then the figure disappeared.

"It sure looked like him. What do you think that was about?" she asked.

"Don't know. Maybe his spirit is looking out for us," I said.

"That's comforting. Could be he's in trouble and needs us. We should talk with Hiram about it, and definitely Grandmother Molly."

"That's a good idea," I replied.

"Where's Uncle Amos and Louis?" she asked. "I thought they were right behind us."

I looked back. "I think I see them coming down the hill. Turn on the lights so they'll see us here." Abby snapped on the lights. It wasn't until then we realized how lucky we were. There was a huge old stump just a couple of feet in front of us. Amos turned on his headlights, and came to a stop right behind us. I could smell his hot brakes. His load was even heavier than ours. Louis hopped out.

"What're you doing?" he shouted. "The road's over there," Louis pointed with a smile. "What happened? You okay?" Uncle Amos shouted out from the cab, the engine's clattering nearly drowning out his soft voice.

"Very funny, Louis," I shot back. "We nearly went through the windshield." I was still rubbing my head where a good size goose egg was forming.

"No brakes," Abby said. "Emergency failed, too."

"Not good," Louis said. "Think we can pull you out? There's got to be a good chain in one of these somewhere."

Louis walked back to their truck, opened the cab door and rummaged behind the seat. Soon, he had a heavy chain in his hands, rattling out of the cab. Uncle Amos turned their truck around and backed up to the edge of the gravel, six feet from our rear bumper. Louis hooked onto our rear frame and then onto the rear frame of Uncle Amos' truck. Abby joined him, watching to see if any shorter logs of the corduroy road pivoted up to catch the frame as we rolled over them.

"I'm putting it in bull low," Uncle Amos said. "Be ready to put it in reverse when you start to move but not sooner. I don't want you to dig any deeper." And with that, Uncle Amos took up the slack from the tow chain as he moved forward. Just as soon as the chain was about to become taught, he gunned his motor and we began to move. Our spinning wheels helped back us right out of the little marsh to the middle of the road. We stepped out of the truck, the chain still taught, and our rear bumper bent out of shape.

"Are we going to make this delivery on time?" Abby asked.

"Maybe," Uncle Amos said. We'll travel behind your bumper

with the chain connecting us. We'll keep it slack for the flats and up the hills, but for the downhills I'll be your brakes. I'll just shift down to bull low and be your anchor. You'll be fine, okay?" Uncle Amos seemed unconcerned about possible risks.

"Okay," we said together. Abby and I crawled back in the truck while Uncle Amos turned his around again. Louis secured the chain between us, then hopped in with Amos. He had made extra wraps around to make sure the chain didn't come off. Then we were on our way, our boots covered with mud and a bruise on my forehead.

We knew we wouldn't be able to fix the brakes. When they go out, they're done and parts would be needed to make them right. We'd have to look at it when we got back to the Dam – IF we got back to the Dam. There were several more turns ahead of us, sharper and steeper than the first two.

An hour later, we were on level ground. Next was the Canadian Pacific siding at the Atlas plywood mill where the private train was waiting for us. Going down hills was a challenge for Uncle Amos. He kept overheating, and we had to stop to cool off at the bottom of the longest hills. By the time we got down Blair Hill, we were both steaming pretty bad. We stopped beside a spring just off the road in a little turn out. After a cool down and more water, we headed for the train which we could almost see along the mill spur.

"There's the train," I said. "I think that's the road down to it." Abby turned in, Uncle Amos still being our brakes, chain still holding, and soon we were in the mill's freight yard, the private train and boxcar waiting for us. There was one street light on the next corner over. We were on time. Two men came out and motioned for us to back up to the boxcar's door. Amos got out and told them about the brakes. Louis unhooked us after chocking our wheels. Then Amos backed up to the door.

We unloaded Uncle Amos first. This was so much easier; no ramp was needed for the barrels. We slid the cases from the truck's deck to the boxcar's floor. When the last barrel was rolled out, Uncle Amos moved his truck away. Abby backed up to the boxcar as Amos pushed against our front bumper. Louis and I checked to see if the bumpers were even. It would be bad if one bumper slid over the other. When the truck came up against the open sliding door of the boxcar, I waved and Uncle Amos put on his brakes. Abby shut off the motor after Louis and I slid some blocks in front of her rear wheels.

When we finished unloading our truck, we reconnected the

chain and readied to make a stop at the building we were renting for a storehouse. Uncle Amos thought there was a spare truck parked there.

"How do we get paid?" I asked Uncle Amos. He was about to answer when a well-dressed man with a sharp, hawkish face approached us in the lead truck. I was at the wheel.

"Mr. King?" he asked before he saw who I was. Some say I look like Father from behind. I nodded.

"I'm John Martin," the portly man said. He was well-dressed, wearing a black and white checkered suit and vest. His wing-tip shoes were light brown with cream-colored saddles that seemed to glimmer in the truck's headlights. His bowler hat covered a balding head. A fancy handkerchief hung out of his breast pocket, and the cigarette he had been smoking was in his left hand between two yellow-stained fingers.

"Mr. Martin?" I asked. "The Mr. Martin of the Company?" There was a John Martin who was a Company official.

"The same. I need to speak with you about the next order."

"You want to speak with my father, Caleb. His brother, Amos, is in the truck behind us." I pointed, shut off the truck and put the transmission in gear to prevent it from rolling away. Abby and I got out to walk back to Uncle Amos with Mr. Martin.

Mr. Martin introduced himself to Uncle Amos and Louis and then praised our brand so much we were becoming a little embarrassed. He handed Uncle Amos a thick envelope. "For your product and a thousand deposit on same order same time and place next month." Uncle Amos opened the envelope and counted the money.

"You're short two hundred," Uncle Amos said, turning his head a little to one side as if to get a better view of Mr. Martin's reddening face. "The deal was for six large delivered. There's sixty-eight here if you include the deposit for the next delivery" He waved the handful of bills at Mr. Martin. "You're short."

'Oh, my, I-I must have miscounted. Here." He reached into his coat pocket, his hands unsteady "Two more bills. Sorry." He handed them to Uncle Amos with an apologetic look, a look that was more fear. Apparently, the King family was getting a reputation of fair but tough to deal with. Don't cross them.

"I'll tell Caleb, but I won't guarantee the same price or a delivery date in a month without talking with him." There was no smile in Uncle Amos' voice or on his face. "How do I get a message to you?"

"Call the main number and ask for me. The operator will connect you to my office," Mr. Martin explained.

"Okay, then. We're off," Uncle Amos said. And with that, Uncle Amos and Louis turned and walked back to their truck. We were getting into ours when Mr. Martin shouted out, "Nice to meet you," and waved at Uncle Amos' backside. Abby rolled her eyes as she turned to get back in the cab. I shook my head, and by the time I was back in the driver's seat, Mr. Martin was back in his private Pullman. As we drove away, the train began pulling out of the short siding.

We stopped at our storehouse by the mill to load up more supplies for the hungry stills. Uncle Amos opened the padlock and we slid the huge barn door open. Towering over the extra truck were sacks of sugar and corn. There were 40-gallon barrels of molasses stacked two high.

"How much of this do we have to take back?" I asked Uncle Amos.

"As much as we can load on. Let's start with the molasses." Uncle Amos and Abby lit three barn lanterns while Louis and I wrestled barrels up on the back of the spare truck.

"Hey, Uncle Amos," I cried to him. He looked up, a sack of sugar in his arms and a question on his face. "Let's be sure this truck runs before we put anything more on it!" Uncle Amos jumped into the cab, Louis cranked, and in a moment the truck fired right up. It took two more hours to load everything up. Both trucks looked like they would buckle under their loads.

We drove the loaded trucks out of the storage building. I turned our brakeless wagon around and backed it inside.

"I'm taking a look at those brakes," Louis said and slid under the middle of the truck with a flashlight. It didn't take long. "Someone's been messing with the brake linkage. The metal rod that makes them work had been cut nearly through." He crawled out from under. "It took only a couple of peddle pushes to break it the rest of the way."

"We'll change the locks on the barn at the Dam before we head back up the lake," Uncle Amos said as he slid the door closed. After he and Louis got in, Abby and I followed them out the little street to Lily Bay Road and up Blair Hill.

First light was breaking over Katahdin when we reached the landing at Chesuncook Dam. I said a silent welcome to the Day Traveler. Hiram recently reminded me of the importance of greeting the dawn properly. But today my greetings were only thoughts wishing us a safe trip. A few hours later, we were parked by the float where *The Twilight* waited. Uncle Amos backed down to the gangplank first.

We were about to load *The Twilight*, when I noticed Abby

standing still, staring at the truck. "I could almost see it happen," she said, "hurtling off the cliff." She turned to Uncle Amos. "I'd like to know why someone tried to get us killed," Abby stared at him.

Uncle Amos always gave straight answers. "Competition, Abby. Maybe not from a big outfit, but hard to say. It's more about the delivery than it is about you." That got me thinking.

"Who'd lose if that delivery wasn't made? Who'd win?" I asked.

"Caleb's been poking his nose into the Boston territory. They go up as far as Old Orchard Beach!" Uncle Amos paused. "They don't want the competition, but they're not the only ones. Who'd win? Whoever could fill the contract."

"But who could do that in short notice?" Abby asked.

"I suppose the Boston market is pretty well matched in supply and demand. I don't think there's much extra moonshine floating around," Uncle Amos explained.

"If someone had a good stock of our product, any product, that person could meet the order we didn't deliver on?" Something wasn't right.

"Remember the Munster clan?" Uncle Amos asked.

"Yeah, they had a farm over on Gero," I recalled.

"Not only a farm, but they had a barge they used for hauling freight up from the Dam. There was a little shack on the barge. They would row or pole it here and there. Once they put a headworks on it." Amos had used a headworks more than one time until steam powered sidewheelers took over. The headworks was a raft with a huge capstan winch in the center, several poles sticking out like spokes for the men to turn. A length of one thousand feet of rope in hundred-foot coils was hooked on to a raft of logs behind. The men used a bateau to row out an anchor as far as the rope would allow and then drop the anchor. The raft was tied to the boom of logs, another rope ahead between the capstan winch and the anchor. The men would walk in circles around that capstan winch, winding up the rope until the raft was pulled up to the anchor. Then they'd repeat the process, sometimes walking around that capstan most of the night.

"I heard talk about that," Abby said. "Didn't they have a still or something on the barge?"

"They sure did," Uncle Amos said. "They even had a sign that said 'The Temple of Knowledge.' But the competition didn't like that idea much."

"The competition? You mean Father?"

"I do. One night, when they got pretty drunk sampling their own hooch and had all passed out, Caleb paddled over in a canoe and cut the ropes that held the raft together. The raft fell apart, sending the cook shack and the Munster boys into the drink before your father got his canoe back to the dock."

"What happened to them?" I asked. Uncle Amos just shook his head.

"We didn't have to dig any graves the next day, but those boys were pretty lucky not to have ended up in one." Amos put his gloves in his back pocket. "They left town, the lot of 'em, and good riddance, too. Too many things had been disappearing around here ever since they first showed up."

"Our brakes failed at just the wrong time," Abby pointed out.

"It would be pretty hard to figure just when that linkage would break," Amos said.

"But if we crashed and burned either before or after the delivery, then could Mr. Martin make up the loss?" Abby asked.

"Maybe not. We'd already brought him over 100 cases," Amos stopped to fill his pipe. "What I don't get is what connections this guy might have with Boston."

"Easy," I said. "Company offices are right on Tremont Street. Father mentioned there was a secret liquor warehouse the next street over. He has had the opportunity to make connections."

"I think we should watch out for Mr. Martin," Abby said. I understood that my own father would put my life in danger, but Abby.... well had anything happened to her, that's another matter.

"Good idea to be extra careful with him when we make his delivery next month. Caleb won't turn it down, I'm afraid." Uncle Amos took the sack of grain I held for him and stacked it with the rest. Louis grabbed the next one from the float, then Abby, then me again. Uncle Amos liked stowing the freight so the boat would be properly balanced. The Day Traveler was climbing over Mt. Katahdin. We were nearly finished when Father rode into the yard. He hopped off his mare and led her to the barn for the stable hand to feed her and brush her down. He then hefted his valise and walked it to the boat for us to load.

"How'd it go?" Father asked Louis. Abby was handing me sacks of corn meal. I balanced a sack on the gunwale until Uncle Amos came over to grab it. Louis was loading crates of empty bottles closer to the stern. Between the bottles and sacks of corn, we kept Uncle Amos hopping.

"We had trouble with the brakes, but everything worked out okay," Louis reported. Uncle Amos added a few more details. Father seemed unconcerned.

"You got paid okay?" Father asked.

"It's in the wheelhouse safe," Uncle Amos said, pointing to the cabin of *The Twilight*. "Martin was short, but corrected his 'mistake.' We switched trucks, loaded supplies and here we are. I don't think we should take that road again," he opined, "and I changed the lock on the barn here to keep the trucks safe. We shouldn't be selling to Martin. It's too risky."

"When I want your opinion, I'll ask for it," Father snapped. "A smarter man would have checked the brakes before even leaving here." He turned away leaving the four of us realizing how expendable we were. Uncle Amos scowled. Father was oblivious to what had almost happened on the Devil's Staircase. So much for family. Anger was growing inside me. Abby sensed what I was feeling. She came behind me, put her arms tightly around my waist, and soon the south wind dropped off.

We loaded the rest of the cargo and followed Father's path to the kitchen. There was so much food left on the table. Scrambled eggs, bacon, biscuits and donuts, flapjacks, pancakes, maple syrup and of course a big bowl of baked beans. The lumbermen had left for the day only moments before. We had the dining room and the leftovers all for ourselves. It was great!

Father told us a little about his trip. He had arranged to supply two repackaging factories all the quality, tax free alcohol they could afford to buy. We already had more orders than we could fill, that is, until the three new stills were assembled and put into production. A second supply run would now be added each week

Soon we were on our way up the lake. There had to be a reckoning, and soon. I didn't see how it all could go on uninterrupted. That an executive of the Company was involved perplexed me. Mr. Martin was probably working on his own, having found a way to make a lot of money on the side. The Boston Gang would not welcome another seller in their market. Maybe the brake problem on the Devil's Staircase had to do with the sale to Mr. Martin. That would make sense. And Father must have had a suspicion at least. I could hear the wind whooshing through the feathers of black wings as the reckoning approached.

The Nest
Chapter 4

"We're going to do this, right Charlie?" Abby asked. We were cleaning out Thunder and Lightning's stall while Amos had them out moving a building across town.

"We are," I said and threw another forkful of ox-stall mess down the open trap door. Below us in the low drive was a wagon. After it filled, we would hook up Duke and drive the wagon out from under to dress the fields that had been left fallow.

"Do you think we can find the old nest? The forest is so different now," Abby said.

"I'm pretty sure we can find the way, but some of the path is under water now. We'll have to pick it up on the other shore," I explained.

"I don't remember hiking through wet places," Abby said.

"Water is twenty-eight feet higher now, remember?"

"That would do it," she said. The dam at the foot of the lake had been rebuilt several times, each reconstruction flooding more and more land. Ripogenus Dam, built just a few years ago, flooded out the cemetery and the homes on Goose Grass Flats. After I tossed the last forkful down the hole to the wagon, Abby closed the trap door, and we climbed up to the loft above the ox pen. Bales of hay were stacked everywhere. These were cut last summer, and the leftover hay had to last until the first mow. Abby and I slid a bale over the floor, opened up the narrow trap door along the back wall and with one leg, pushed the hay down to the racks below.

"When do you want to go? It wouldn't take all day, would it?" she asked.

"Let's go tomorrow. We're caught up on chores. Okay with you?" I replied.

"That's good," she said. We climbed down into the ox pen.

"I was thinking about Moosis in war paint. I think of it a lot," I said.

"Me too," Abby replied. "I think he was trying to tell us something." We walked back to the house and made our plans to be away the next day as long as the weather would hold. Uncle Amos let us use his small skiff.

....

The next morning, we left the village cove with Abby in the stern and me at the oars. She was directing. We could smell the newly exposed mud flats baking in the hot sun.

"Over that way a little, Charlie," she'd say, waving her hand to one side or the other. A rower often faces the stern of the boat and has to turn around from time to time to see where the bow is headed. It's easier to pull on the oars than to face forward and push. Having Abby in the stern meant all I had to do was follow orders. It would have been a faster trip if she had a rudder. After an hour of following her directions, we touched the shore where the old path had been. Even though the old path was long gone, critters made a trail that led to the same general area.

We reached a flat place where the loggers hadn't yet cut. Tall pines swayed above us.

"Nothing looks right," I said. "Isn't the aerie on the other side of that ridge?" I pointed to the undulating line of bushy green tree tops ahead of us.

"I thought it was on this side. I remember it being closer," Abby remarked. "The new shoreline makes things harder to recognize."

We followed a path that ran parallel to the shoreline of Caucmagomic Stream. It wasn't long before we could see part of the cliff we were going to climb jutting out between the bushy tops.

"This is right, Charlie. I can feel it," Abby said.

"You mean over there? The cliff looks a lot different." I waved my arm toward the rocks. "It looks like some of the rock face has fallen away." Abby was silent. "Abby?" She was standing still, right behind me staring into the forest. She was shaking.

"Abby, what's wrong?" I asked. She didn't respond. "Abby?" Abby stared into the distance.

"Do you see him?" She asked quietly,

"See who?" I asked.

"There. By those boulders," she pointed.

A mist hovered, and as the wind began to disperse it, a figure was taking shape. A young brave, face covered in war paint and carrying a spear, stood in front of us. It was the same figure we had seen on the Devil's Staircase. At first, he walked right toward us and stood, or should I say floated, a few feet away. Black feathers hung from the spear shaft. On its tip was lashed a spear point of Munsungan chert, bands of black, green and cream from side to side. The figure motioned for us to follow and disappeared between the trees.

"Moosis?" I asked.

"Must be," Abby said. "We should follow him."

"I wonder what he's leading us to," I said. Moosis' spirit beckoned us on, and we followed the shifting mist into the woods. "Did you see the spear point? It looks just like the one he gave me."

"He seemed to be pointing to it. I don't see him anymore. Where'd he go?" Abby asked.

"I don't know, but look where he's led us. Remember squeezing up that crevasse?" I pointed to the cliff ahead. "This is where we started climbing to the nest to rescue Little Rabbit, remember?"

"What do you think we'll find when we get there?" Abby asked as she peered through the alder bushes at the climb ahead.

"Part of me hopes we don't find a thing." The last time we were in the aerie was when I fought Blackfeather, who morphed into Ki'kwa'jenu as the raptor fell backwards from the cave towards the rocks below, spreading its black wings and flying off into the dark.

It was a tougher climb than before. Over the centuries, several large boulders had tumbled into the crevasse, some of the roof had collapsed and climbing around the debris was challenging. We didn't see Moosis' spirit again. A new opening in the cave's roof let in more light. The boulder we had hid behind was in the same place. We snuck up behind it as before, peering around the sides to check out the aerie. In the center were the remains of a giant nest, some larger pieces of wood still here and there that outlined the original shape. This couldn't have been the original nest material; that would have disintegrated long ago. This nest was from something more recent. The front edge of the cliff had broken off some time ago. Thick moss grew along the edge. There were no bones. Time and field mice had taken care of those.

"The aerie looks empty," Abby said. We stood at the back of the cavern. "Should we go all the way in?" she asked.

"Definitely," I said. "It doesn't look like it's been used for a long time, but I want to be sure." We came around the boulder and walked around the outside ring of the old nest area. Cobwebs were everywhere. Recent Nighthawk tracks or claw marks would really show up, but there were none. Bats had taken up residence in a darker nook along the side by the looks of guano that lead from the cave's mouth. The odor almost knocked me over.

"Looks like the Nighthawk is living somewhere else," Abby said. I was examining the mouth of the aerie, finding no indications of a recent Ki'kwa'jenu visit. There were no eggs in the nest, no broken shells, no feathers, no shiny objects and no bones. I wouldn't have expected it to be any different after all those centuries, but I had to know if it was being used by the beast that was still tracking me.

"But 'where' is the question now," I said. "Maybe it's 'when,' too," I added. I moved to the side of the nest. "Wait, what's this?" I bent over to pick up some lighter colored stones. These were small, flat and round pieces about the size of a dime. There was a small hole in each one. These had been strung together and worn as a necklace.

"Who wore these?" I wondered aloud. Abby knew as much as I did. One of Ki'kwa'jenu's victims had worn these.

"I don't know, but if we could take them back to Grey Wolf's village, we could find out," she said.

"Maybe not a good idea to mix up artifacts in the wrong timestreams," I pointed out as I put them back in the dust. "These were strung together with a strip of deer hide and decorated some important person's neck. They might already exist back then. If we bring them back, there'll be two sets." Then I saw a spear point, then another, and another beside that. "Look, Abby. Look at all the spear points. Some are broken, too!"

"This means there was a fight here, several throwing spears."

"I count five spear points in this area alone." That would mean five men unless someone carried a spare in case there was a larger, more dangerous quarry they were after. "It looks like a war party was after the Nighthawk in its own aerie."

"I wonder who won." Abby sniffed the air, wrinkling her nose. "It really smells in here."

"What I'd really like to know is how the Nighthawk is able to follow me across time. Does it live here now, or does it somehow bridge the centuries when I see its red eyes glowing at me?"

"Since Moosis' spirit can transcend those years, I'm not surprised the Nighthawk can, too," Abby said.

"We should go," I said. "At least we know its current nest is not in this aerie. And there's no treasure either."

"Let's get out of this stinky cave." Abby was holding her nose. "Nothing has been here for a very long time, and it smells really bad." I agreed, and we left the aerie, climbing down the cleft in the rocks in silence.

"Please pass the canteen," Abby asked. After we climbed to the bottom of the pile of scree, we sat to enjoy the view down the lake. "Let's say we go back to Grey Wolf's village, and travel here with a hunting party to fight the Nighthawk. Wouldn't we remember being there?"

"Maybe," I offered. "But our presence would create only a slight ripple in the timestream. If we do go back and join that fight, when we return home and re-visit the aerie where we found the broken spear points, we'd remember what happened."

"I think you're right," Abby said. I smiled, not hearing her say that often. "I wonder if the Nighthawk is still terrorizing villages. That might explain the broken points and loose beads."

There was no other sign of Moosis as we made our way through the old resting place. On our last trip here, long ago, we had to duck under the platforms where tribal remains were wrapped in animal hides, dodging strafing runs from Ki'kwa'jenu. On this trip, it was just another flat area in the forest, partially flooded out by Rip Dam.

A stiff breeze came up when we got to the skiff. We rowed out of Caucmagomic Stream into Chesuncook Lake, the wind pushing us along. I thought about the Objibwe saying: "Sometimes I go about in pity for myself, and all the while, a great wind carries me across the sky."

Jim Ross
Chapter 5

It was a mirror calm evening when *The Twilight* slid up beside its dock in the village cove. A Canada Dry ginger ale crate was upside down near the edge of the float. Blind Bill, one of our neighbors, would sit on that crate for hours with his alder rod catching fish for the cats and Heidrick, a friendly Australian Shepherd. When Bill felt a fish on the line, he'd jerk the pole in the air, sending the fresh catch flying onto the lawn behind him, the fish flopping free of the hook most of the time. Heidrick didn't always get to the prize. Sometimes one of the cats pounced on it and dragged the wriggling fish safely into the bushes or under the screened-in porch for a private snack. After a few days in the hot sun, even Blind Bill would nose the remains, which he would toss into the lake.

The boat came alongside the float. Louis, Abby and I wrangled the lines and bumpers. A few river drivers gathered their gear, slung driving boots over shoulders, and waited to load the smaller boat for the last leg of their trip to the Upper Boom House just below Pine Stream Falls. Others were lodging with us at the Inn.

Waiting to step over the gunwale and onto the dock, a man in bare feet stood beside a large wooden box. He was tall and thin as a rail, wearing only a shirt and pants. A cord of twine served as a belt. 'BIBLES' was stenciled on the side of the box, and the name of the company that printed them: 'Holy Word Press, 1 Church Street, Charleston, SC.' Funny thing was, this was really a crate of bibles and not bottles of *Tanglefoot* being transported by moonshiners.

"Hand me that box, Charlie," Louis said. He was on the float stacking supplies in the wheelbarrow that Uncle Amos would push to the truck at the end of the gangplank. I hefted the box of bibles. The minister stepped onto the dock, no suitcase in sight. When Louis hefted the crate, he looked puzzled.

"How come nothing's clinking inside here?" Louis asked the man. "Did you use hay or something to deaden the sound?" The minister made no reply, I think because he didn't understand the reference. Louis smiled and took the crate to the wagon. He had a smart mouth sometimes.

Next to be unloaded was a heavy trunk. "Be careful of that trunk," I heard a voice behind me as I dragged it over the gunwales and onto the float. It was the shoeless minister who had hitched a ride. "I'm staying at the Katahdin View Inn," he said. "Can you tell me where it is?"

"That's the place," I said, pointing to our Inn. "I'll get your things there for you."

"Thank you, young man," he said. Maybe I could interest you in a bible later, or maybe a nice cross for your dresser?" He held up a gaudy cross with red, blue and green jewels of different sizes, all certainly glass.

"Umm, sure, we'll have to leave the trunk in the woodshed with the others." The last thing I wanted was a bible. But the cross gave me an idea. I handed the next box to Louis. He and Abby stacked it all in the back of the wagon. With the three of us passing boxes and bibles, we were done in no time. Except for the last thing, a huge round wooden tub, two iron bands holding it together, "Maple Sugar" the label read.

Louis and Abby helped me roll the heavy tub up a plank and down to the dock, then up the gangplank to shore and into the back of the wagon with all the rest. Abby slapped the reins on Duke's back, and they lumbered to the Cunningham Barn.

"Help me slide this skiff in the water. These men need to get up river," Father bellowed. I trudged over.

"Maybe we could keep this afloat? It's pretty heavy," I suggested.

"That ain't a boat," Father grumbled, "It's a damned floating vegetable!" Apparently, this skiff didn't handle so well. It was so heavy that it took four of us to grunt it into the water. "Take the supplies to the Cunningham Barn," Father said before leaving. He didn't seem to care that Abby was already on her way there. I think he expected me to run after her with these orders as if I didn't have a suspicion about where we kept these supplies. This barn was by far the largest in our village. From the cupola I could see all the way down to Ripogenus. We had a lease on it for the next five years. Because it was on the lot next to the Inn, Father and Amos wanted to buy it, but the lease was the best we could do for now. We got the supplies into the old barn, and soon arrived back at the Inn for lunch. We'd unload the coffin, Bibles and the rest after we ate. Olive greeted us as we came into the kitchen.

"Hey, Olive," I said. "What's new and exciting?"

She motioned to the kitchen table. Sitting at the end, eating a donut, was what looked to be a boy about twelve. "Say hello, Erik," she said.

"Hi," the boy said. I was so stunned I couldn't speak. Sitting at our kitchen table was Moosis. Of course, I knew it couldn't be Moosis, but Erik looked just like him except for the hair color. "Hi," I said. "Welcome to the Katahdin View Inn."

Abby seemed surprised, too. "Hey, Erik. Nice to meet you," she said when she found her voice. The boy stood up. His frame was huge. He was at that age when his body was growing out of control and nothing seemed to match. He was growing into his hands and feet, already as large as mine. His flaming red hair made him stand out even more. It looked like Moosis was in our kitchen, minus the face paint and deerskin clothing.

"What do you need for help?" I asked Olive.

"Firewood, dishes, and see if you can dig out some potatoes and onions from the root cellar. We're having stew tonight," she replied. "Charlie, take Erik with you so he'll know where things are. He'll be staying with us for the summer."

"Okay, Erik, let's get going," I said. I set my pack basket down, motioning for the boy to follow me to the firewood pile in the connecting shed. We were packing the last armful into the woodbox when I heard a dog barking. It didn't sound like Heidrick. I looked out the screen door to see a large man walking across the lawn to the porch, a big black dog beside him.

"Abby!" I called. "Can you come to the door? Someone's here." I stepped aside so she could see. The screen door flung open, Abby rushed by me with a squeal of delight and jumped into the stranger's arms.

"Dad," she cried out. "You didn't tell me you were coming back so soon!" She buried her face into his green plaid shirt, drawing her long arms around him. The black dog jumped up on her.

"Okay, kid, you're squeezing the wind out of me," he finally said as she released her iron grip from his waist, moving to his arm. "Didn't have time to let you know," he finally said. "This is Bear Dog," pointing to the black dog who was now tongue washing happy tears from Abby's face.

"Oh, hey, Bear Dog," Abby said to him, scratching his ears. Where'd you get this guy?"

"Out west just before I started back. He's good company as long as he doesn't get into a skunk. And who's this?" he asked, nodding in my direction.

"Charlie, this is my Dad, Jim Ross," she explained. I reached out my hand and it disappeared in his giant mitt. The country's most famous river driver pumped it up and down.

"Abby's written about you, Charlie. Good to meet you," he said.

"Nice to meet you," I replied. "Staying with us?"

"That would be good," Jim said. "Our old camp just up river has a tree through the roof. One of last winter's wind storms uprooted a huge red spruce that crushed part of the roof. Broken boards and shingles were letting in the weather and the skeeters and we couldn't stay there."

"Oh no!" Abby exclaimed. "The camp was fine when we were up river last month."

"It can be fixed easy enough," Jim said. "Any chance for a late breakfast?" he asked.

"I'll get you something," Abby said. "This is Olive, and that tiny guy over there is Erik," she explained. Erik blushed a bit. Jim said hello to Olive and walked over to shake Erik's hand.

"Make yourself at home," Olive said. Jim pulled up a seat at the kitchen table. "When did you come East?" she asked. Abby's father was the best-known river boss in the East. When the woodland owners in Oregon found out about him, he traveled there to show them how to move logs down streams, ponds, lakes and rivers.

"After I brought the drive into their giant mill pond, I took a train to Bangor," he explained, "and came right up after a short stop in Greenville. There was a rough boat ride from Kineo to Northeast Carry, and a rocky barge ride down the river to the Boom House below Pine Stream Falls. We walked from there, didn't we, Bear Dog?" Jim reached down and ruffled Bear's ears. The Great Pyrenees wagged his tail, begged to go out, and was soon running around the yard where he and Heidrick took turns chasing each other, marking every tree and bush they could find.

Jim, settled at the extended lunch table, was about to take a sip of his coffee when Abby's Aunt Rose came into the kitchen. She was our school teacher and looked after Abby when her father was away.

"I thought I heard a familiar voice," she cried from the living room and soon after warm greetings, sat down to join her brother at the table. "How have you been? Have you come to stay a while?" Jim got up and gave her a big hug.

"Couldn't be better, Rose," Jim said. "It was a good spring drive. We got all the logs to market, and I'm here for a nice, long rest. Come, sit down. Here's a place for you."

"I can stay only a moment. The sewing circle is about to start its meeting. We're making a wedding quilt for the next lucky couple." She took the seat her brother offered.

"Charlie, where's your father?" Olive asked.

"Coming back from the Boom House," I said. "He should be back soon unless he had to go to Black Pond to check on our logs. Come on, Erik. There's a garden that needs hoeing."

Abby visited with her father while Erik and I got another chore crossed off the morning's list. The bugs weren't too bad; a sharp northeast wind kept most at bay.

"Where's home?" I asked him. "Take one of those hoes." I waved my hand at the gardening tools hung up in shed as we went to the garden. I grabbed one on the way by, and Erik did the same.

"Nicatou," he said. That was Grandmother Molly's home village, her 'Ndakina.'

"We've been there," I said. "It's pretty nice. I don't remember meeting you then."

"I came to stay with my cousins last month, but I got sick. Olive came and got me as soon as I was better," he explained.

"Did you meet Grandmother Molly and Hiram?" I asked. Abby's Grandmother Molly and Hiram were a couple. Although he enjoyed his solitude at his Village cabin, he was spending more time with her at Nicatou.

"I did. Grandmother Molly is the one who got me better, and Hiram can tell a good story."

"He certainly can. We've learned a lot from him." I didn't want to go into any detail until I got to know Erik a little better. "Where are your folks?"

"There was an accident," he said. "The boat that was taking them across Chamberlain Lake went down. No one survived."

"I'm so sorry to hear that," I said. I knew that later on we'd talk about how *The Tethys* I was on blew up and seventeen migrant workers lost their lives. There were fatal accidents every year, but I hadn't heard of this one. I'd have to ask Uncle Amos.

"You take the rows of peas, and I'll do the beans, okay?"

"Sure," he agreed. We hoed up weeds for a while until we heard the shuttle boat chug into the cove. It wasn't long before Father came across the lawn. We thought it would be a good time to take a break, so we went back through the wood shed and into the kitchen for a drink. Jim, Abby and Rose were having coffee. In walked Father, stopping in his tracks when he saw who was sitting at the table with Abby and Rose. Erik and I had already come inside.

"Jim! Good to see you, you old pole-cat. You're just in time." He walked over, hands were shaken, and soon Father had a steaming cup of fresh coffee in his hand.

"In time for what?" Jim asked.

"In time to get our winter's cut off the river bank and floating to market. Interested in helping out?"

"Interested? Couldn't keep me away from a drive. You know that, Caleb!" Jim sat down.

"Of course, there's money in it, right? I do have a reputation to keep up, you know."

Father just smiled and nodded. "I'll take care of you, Jim. I have some very special reserve, aged a couple of years now."

"Now, Caleb," Jim said, "I don't usually work for booze. I thought you knew that. Cash money. And I think you can afford it, too." Father's cigar was beginning to act like a worm, wriggling from side to side. "Although I have heard you make the best in two counties!" Father stopped playing with his cigar stub.

"I've put a crew together, and tomorrow morning we're heading to Caucmagomic Stream to start the drive," Father explained. "You'll be leading them.

"Getting a little late, Caleb, water-wise I mean?" Jim asked.

"Getting close," Father replied. "There's enough water still upstream so we can open the squirt dam and flush them down to Black Pond and then warp them down to First Falls. It's the last of the logs to come down this year. After next week, there won't be enough water." One season, Father and Amos had to leave part of a winter's work rotting in the woods when the water finally drained out of Caucmagomic Lake. It was their own fault, having waited too long to get it going. The bugs got in the wood, and no one wanted to buy boards with worm tracks all through them.

"Sounds good, Caleb. Maybe I should work for my keep?" Jim asked.

"Okay, plus a dollar a day?"

"Not when everyone else is getting a buck fifty!" Jim replied. "And I don't do any time on the headworks, either." He must have known that Father was cheap and wouldn't hire a boat to tow his boom of logs. He'd hire men to slave on the headworks instead and pay them in *Tanglefoot*.

"You're always such a tough man to make a deal with," Father said. "We could trade your expert advice for putting you up?"

"Or putting up with me, don't you mean?" Jim said with a smile. "Okay, we have a deal. When do we start?"

"First light in the morning. We're all going up. Olive will set up a kitchen at the Black Pond Depot."

"Charlie, you and your buddy need to get tomorrow's gear together. And don't forget the extra rope. We may need it to tie off the boom before we're done." He hadn't been introduced to Erik and saw him as just another pair of hands waiting to help. That was Father.

Erik, Abby and I spent the rest of the morning loading up *The Twilight* for the trip up river. Olive called us in for lunch. We were at the table and Olive had just finished serving dessert, a lemon cake.
Then Jim dropped the bomb that was going to destroy my life.

"After we get your logs down to the mouth of the river, Abby and I are going to Quebec."

Everyone stopped moving as the second hand on the kitchen clock ticked ahead.

"Quebec?" Abby asked.

"The convent runs a good school there, and I've made all the arrangements." He shoveled in another forkful of mashed potato, peering at Abby under his bushy eyebrows. Except for the water heating on the stove, there was no sound in the kitchen. Then I understood that Abby's father was just like mine, controlling and arrogant.

"No, not the convent's boarding school!" Abby shouted. Her tone made it sound like 'anything but that place!'

"I know you didn't like it when you were there before, but then you were much younger. After a while, you'll get to like it," Jim said.

"Maybe after a hundred years," Abby sassed back. "I'm going to be eighteen this fall and can decide for myself, no matter where I might be then." She threw her napkin down as she kicked over her chair with a crash, dropped her plate into the sink somehow without breaking it and stormed out of the kitchen through the back door, slamming it behind her. Jim Ross kept chewing his steak. I excused myself. There was only a raised eyebrow from Father. Olive was examining the rim around her plate, and Rose seemed to be staring out the window, or maybe it was at the window.

"You'll have to excuse me," Rose said as she stood. "The sewing circle is starting. We'll catch up at dinner?" Jim, his mouth full, nodded his head and waved his hand as she turned and walked out by the front porch.

I found Abby sitting on a bale of hay just inside the barn. She was scattering corn for the chickens. Her face was wet.

"Charlie, what are we going to do?" she asked as I reached out for her. There were tears in her eyes as I held her. The south wind was beginning to rise until I realized that Abby was shaking me, "Charlie, it's me. Stop! You have to relax! Please?" Around the time my semi-focused brain processed the "please," one tree on the point had already fallen with sounds of snapping limbs filling the air. I began to relax. The wind calmed down. No one came outside from the Inn to check. They knew about my relationship with Sowanakik and that only Abby could calm things down.

"Sorry, I'm just so angry and not just with your father. It's also mine." I relaxed my arms, and we touched our heads together for a moment. I was tired of being treated like a hired hand of no particular value.

"I know, Charlie. They seem so much alike! But he can't send me away. I-I won't let him." When Abby sets her jaw the way it was right now, there was nothing more to be done. Choices had already been analyzed, decisions had been made, but what ones? I wondered. I slid my hands down her arms to her wrists and held her hands.

"Look, let me talk with Rose. Maybe she can convince your father not to send you there," I offered.

"I hope she will, Charlie. I know my father isn't too happy about me helping with the King family business, especially when we nearly got turned into ground meat on the Devil's Staircase," Abby informed me. "I'm sure Aunt Rose told him. And I'd do it all again if I needed to," she added with a squeeze and a warm smile, "as long as we are together." I held her while her breathing calmed.

"Let's go inside," I offered. "We can help Olive clean up the lunch dishes. Maybe folks have calmed down a little."

"Meaning you, Mr. Sowanakik?" She gave me a smile and a big hug, and we walked back to the kitchen, hand in hand, Abby wiping her face.

When we got back inside, Rose was with the sewing circle with the rest of the wedding quilt makers in the meeting house, but Jim and Caleb still sat talking on the porch. Their voices seemed to get louder as they emptied the bottle they were sharing. Olive was cleaning up, and Abby and I helped her finish.

"I don't know if it'll help, but I'll try to reason with Caleb in hopes he's willing to speak with Jim. You're safe here, Abby," Olive said. I didn't think she knew about our daredevil ride the other night, but I'm still wondering how Rose knew.

"Thanks, Olive," Abby smiled at her. "Are we ready for the trip to Black Pond?" Abby seemed more excited now about the drive than when we first learned of it.

"Just about," Olive said. "Just staging the gear and food in the back room. It's all in one pile. You'll see it." We finished up with the dishes and turned to loading up the gear set aside in the pantry. It was almost like moving. At least there was a cast iron cook stove already in place at the Black Pond camps.

Father and Jim rose from the green painted wicker rockers on the porch as Abby, Erik and I returned from loading the last of the gear. Father waved in our direction.

The Last Drive
Chapter 6

I brought Duke to a stop as Father approached the wagon. "We need you to help untangle the tow rope," he said. "The line got wrapped around the engine shaft between the paddle wheel and the hull. It's in there pretty good."

"On *The A.B. Smith*?" I asked.

"That's right," he said. "Jim and I will take you and Abby in the skiff." *The A.B. Smith* was a sidewheeler tow boat and had been working on the lake for over twenty years. Rumors swirled around the possible construction of a larger, more powerful boat to be built at the foot of the lake. These boats towed booms of logs for paper and lumber down the lake to the next dam, Ripogenus. From there, the wood sluiced its way down a concrete gutter, dumping into the gorge. The logs passed through a mile-long narrow canyon of unnavigable whitewater and if they didn't jam up in the Heaters or at the ledge called Troublemaker, they were home free.

"Okay," I said. "We'll see you at the dock." I urged Duke to the barn where we put him in his stall with a snack for a job well done. Abby didn't look too happy.

"Still mad at him?" I asked.

"I'm so mad at him, he's the last person I want to be around right now!" she exploded. Her face was beginning to color, the blood leaving her pursed lips.

"Maybe you should go up river with us in case he has a change of heart and wants to tell you. He couldn't do that if you weren't with us," I pointed out.

"You think so?" She looked up at me. "Maybe I'd have a chance to push him in the river!" I really hoped Abby and her father could mend fences. This tension wasn't good. The spirits were always listening.

"You never know," I said. "Could be he's really sorry but doesn't know how to tell you." Her face seemed to brighten a little. "There's a tow line to untangle, and we'd better get going."

The four of us took the skiff up the river to the first bend. The channel was deepest there, and we could see the tow boat tied to the channel marker, a 30' log with one end sunk deep into the mud. Some called it a "dead man," probably because it didn't have to do much other than stay buried and keep a tow boat in position. *The A.B. Smith*'s bow rope passed through a four-inch hole at the top of the log. Jim tied us to the fantail of the steamer, its smoke stacks pushing wisps of white into the sky.

"Get out the pick-poles," Father said. These eight or ten-foot poles were carried by the river drivers just as much for balance while they ran across floating logs as for the primary tool used to push the logs along the river, around a rock or two. Jim took off his boots and his green plaid wool shirt. Next, he tied a rope around his waist and handed the end to Abby.

"Now's your chance," Jim said and gave her a warm smile. "My life is in your hands." I could tell that Abby wasn't wanting to smile back, but the corners of her mouth were turned up just a bit. She didn't reply.

Abby would feed out the line as he dove around the wheel to where the rope was wrapped around the side drive shaft. Father and I used the pick-poles to push away any stray logs that came careening along the boat's side where he would be working. Jim slid into the cold water, dove under, and came up by the inside of the wheel. He then disappeared into the dark water, a long knife in his teeth.

A few logs floated by, escapees from the boom just around the bend. Father and I pushed them away with no problem. Abby managed the rope, feeding it off the deck as Jim needed more slack. After repeated diving, he had the snarled tow-rope cut away from the wheel's shaft. When Abby felt a tug on the line, she pulled in the rope as her father came to the surface.

"Thanks," he said to Abby on the way back in the skiff. "You had my life in your hands."

"I was tempted to let it go." Abby studied his face for a reaction.

"I can't say that anyone would have blamed you. Maybe we

should start over, you know, back before I brought up that whole Quebec thing." Jim looked at her.

"Really?" she asked.

"Really," Jim replied. "Your Aunt Rose is your greatest admirer. She convinced me that such a move would not be in your best interest. That school isn't such a great idea after all. I think Rose could do as good a job keeping an eye on you. You seem really happy here." He reached out to her, and Abby flew into his wet arms.

"Thanks, Dad," she said. "It means everything to me to be able to stay."

"Okay, let me get into some dry clothes and we'll be off to Black Pond to do some real work!" Abby broke the tension with one of her smiles as she wiped a tear away. It looked like peace had been made. Since it was getting later in the day, Father decided to wait and go to Black Pond in the morning.

We had the rest of the day off. Louis, Anna and the baby joined us for supper. Uncle Amos, Rose and Jim were there, too. Except for Abby's Grandmother Molly and my mentor Hiram, my entire family was at the table. Father had just come in and draped his jacket and hat on the back of one of the kitchen chairs. The rest of us were sitting down in the dining room. Our guests had already been fed, so we had the dining room to ourselves.

Olive brought in a roast followed by Uncle Amos who carried a large yellow bowl of mashed potatoes. The gravy and biscuits were already there.

"This looks great, Olive," Jim said, tucking his napkin under his worn shirt collar as Olive set the platter on the table, spearing a slab of roast beef on the way by. As soon as Uncle Amos pulled up his chair, he picked up the platter and passed it on.

"Now where's that gravy?" Jim asked. He was clearly focused on eating.

"You've seen your share of river driving accidents," Father asked Jim. "What one sticks out to you?" Jim was swallowing a biscuit, whole by the looks of it.

"I'd have to say that would be what happened to the Irishman on Abol Falls," he mused.

"Did it matter that he was Irish?" Abby asked.

"Not really, I guess. Could've happened to a Pollock, too, but they were more cautious as a rule. It was the swearing that sticks out in my mind." Jim speared another slab of roast beef.

"What happened?" I asked.

"This river driver had red hair and swore like a pirate." He turned to Erik. "You're not a pirate, are you Erik?" Jim smiled.

"Not as far as I know," Erik replied sharply. I could tell he was sensitive about his appearance.

Jim continued. "Red may well have been a pirate the way he talked. The boys were driving long logs down Abol Falls when a jam formed around the big Grey rock in the middle of the rapids." Jim wiped his mouth with the napkin still tucked under his chin.

"Red swore to the rest of the crew that he was going to break that jam or he would go to Hell doing it." We all stopped eating and looked at Jim. "Red grabbed a double-bladed ax and scampered over the wet logs to the center of the jam. He chopped and chopped at the king log, the one log that is holding everything back. When it started to crack, that's when the river driver throws the ax and runs for shore like the devil himself was closing in."

"But he didn't throw the ax and run?" Rose asked.

"Oh, he sure did, but just not in time. The pressure that had built up in that log jam all of a sudden let go. The king log he had been chopping at snapped in half well before it was expected to. Red had turned to start running for the river bank as half of it shot out of the pile. That log came after him as fast as lightning. It nailed him right in the small of his back. His head and heels met with an awful sounding crack!"

"Where did they find his body?" I asked. It didn't sound to me as if Red had survived.

"He was never found. Never, not that drive or any time since. Please pass the potatoes." After dumping another pile of potatoes on his large dinner plate, Jim got quiet. I couldn't tell if he was thinking about his meal or the fate of the Irishman. We were all staring at Jim, waiting to hear the end of his story.

"What happened after?" Abby said.

"The usual. We found an old pair of caulked boots and hung them up in the branches of a tree on the shore near where he disappeared. They stayed there for quite a few years after," he explained. Our dinner became rather quiet after that.

. . . .

The next morning, we were up before the sun. Abby poured her father some coffee while Olive got breakfast together. Rose and Erik came to help. We were off in *The Twilight* just as the sun was coming over Mt. Katahdin. The river trip wound us around some foothills on the way to the Black Pond Depot. We pulled into the dock mid-morning and lugged gear up to the camp. Jim gave Rose some extra food for Bear. It was too dangerous around rolling logs and moving water for any dog to be hanging out, so Bear would be staying at the little camp with Rose and Olive and Erik, who stayed to help them get set up. After we got our lunch pails and gear together, we launched the bateau and rowed to the end of the pond, poling it up the narrow channel of Caucmagomic Stream to where our logs were piled on the river bank. This time, Abby drew the short straw and was at the oars. I was smiling in the stern for a change.

Not until we tied up the double-bow boats in an eddy, just below the start of the Oxbow, did we put on our caulked driving boots. Our logs would swing into the current after they were rolled off the shore, drifting around the boats in the eddy current, and floating to the boom bag of long logs that gathered them at the entrance of Black Pond.

"There are a lot more logs than I remember," I said to Uncle Amos, pointing to the log piles that were parallel to the river bank. Everything looked different now, no longer under a blanket of snow and ice.

"The logs pile up pretty fast at cutting time," Uncle Amos replied. "When they're covered with snow, everything seems smaller somehow." His hand waved farther upstream where other rows of saw logs waited to begin their water journey to the sorting booms in Argyle or Old Town, some eighty miles down the river. The "King" symbol, a "K" with a short line under it, was pounded into the end of each log. I was told the line was to separate our "K" from the Kennebec Log Drive "K" that also had the single capital letter stamped on an end of a log. The raised symbol was welded to the head of an ax, and my job had been "branding" all the logs in the piles by swinging the ax head against the end of the logs. By the time we had finished cutting and hauling to the river bank, everything had disappeared under the fresh March snows, and the piles had looked like just part of the river bank.

The crew got to work. Ropes that helped secure the piles were removed, coiled and stacked by the little beach for their ride back to the barn. Then Jim started giving the orders. We could always tell where he was, his booming voice most likely carrying miles through the woods, and if we couldn't hear him, we'd look for his green plaid wood shirt he always wore. His yellow suspenders made him even more visible.

"Set that pile loose first," he said, sending the six-man crew we had assembled at the Village to the pile farthest down-stream. Four men, two on each side, set to chopping away at the "pins," upright posts about eight feet apart that kept the logs from rolling into the water. Wood chips flew in all directions as if a bevy of beavers were building a dam. Soon, one axeman on each side stepped away, leaving the other to finish the job. It was safer not to have one axeman scrambling for safety over another, so two for speed at first, then one for safety.

"Can I chop one of those?" Abby asked.

"You can do the first half of one," Jim replied. "Let's get these going and you can do the last pile." We heard a loud snap! The first holding pin had given way and the last of the two axemen jumped aside, away from any rolling logs. But nothing moved. The entire pile was held back by one pin that was nearly cut through. Then the pin simply exploded. The noise of the rolling logs reverberated through the forest. The last axeman made it to safety, throwing his ax aside to make his escape a little safer.

"That was pretty close," I said.

"It was," agreed Jim. "We lose a lot of axes but he knew what he was doing." The logs seemed to come alive, as if they sensed their new freedom, rolling over each other in a scramble to the water. The dust rose from the writhing pile, and the sun let loose the scent of fresh cut spruce that had been trapped within the pile since March. With a loud splash they rolled into the stream on their way to a boom that would catch them before entering the pond. The rest of the crew began herding the first pile around the corner and returned for the second.

There were so many piles, one so close to the other, there was barely room to pass between them. It was late in the afternoon when we began working on the last one, the largest of all.

"That's a pretty cock-eyed pile," Jim said to Abby. "You'll want to keep an eye on that top log." It seemed to balance as though a clap of thunder could bring it down. "I'll chop the other side." Abby was pretty excited to be helping her father, especially after the "convent" conversation had been resolved. She grabbed her ax. Chips were flying each time Abby's ax connected with the post. She never missed. By the time Jim was halfway through his retaining post, he looked up to see the same thing that we all did. Except Abby. The vibration from all of the ax strikes just below it must have started things. The top log was now teetering at an angle and about to roll down the pile straight for her. Before we could shout, Jim had thrown his ax and dove the rest of the way across the log pile, knocking Abby away from the steamroller that headed her way, pushing her out of danger just in time. There were two loud cracks as the pins shattered under the weight, and the rest of the pile rolled happily into the river, pushing Jim Ross into Caucmagomic Stream with the King family's winter payroll.

"Where is he?" one of the men shouted, stepping on top of a piece of ledge. "Is that his hat over there?" He pointed to a derby hat floating down the river just as it and the logs disappeared around the corner.

Abby was out cold. Uncle Amos and I dragged her farther away from the remaining logs that hadn't made it to the water. I got my canteen so I could splash some water on her face.

"Get the rest of these logs into the water," Father shouted at the men, slack-jawed from what they had just witnessed: the most famous river driver of them all being rolled into the water with the pile of saw logs he was working on. "Go on, get them rolling. It's what you're being paid to do! Christ's underwear! We won't have this water flow for much longer. There's nothing that can help Jim Ross now." Still, two of his crew didn't listen and started hiking across the little tree covered point to check out the logs about to reappear from around the corner. Maybe Jim Ross would be sitting on one of them as it bobbed in the current, swearing a blue streak.

From time to time, we looked to the riverbend for Jim's plaid shirt and yellow suspenders but couldn't see them. I thought he was under the logs, moving in the current and sliding over the smooth rocks on the stream bed.

The two men returned. One was holding a large, torn shirt of green and black plaid wool, part of a yellow suspender snarled around it.

I had my arm around Abby, sitting her up as both of us leaned against one of the logs that refused to go for a swim with his friends. She was coming to.

"What? What happened?" She stood up, winced and put her hand to her left elbow. "Ouch, that hurts! Where's Dad?" Then she saw the river drivers standing in front of her. One of them held her father's dripping wet shirt.

"Sorry, ma'am," the one holding Jim's shirt said. "It's all we found." He carefully set the remains of the shirt on the log beside Abby. "So far," he added. And the realization of what had happened overtook her.

"Dad? Dad!" She screamed at the river as if the current would stop and listen. Abby struggled to stay standing. "No, no, not Dad," she began to sob. I put my arms around her and held her while one of the drivers handed me his handkerchief with brown tobacco juice stains. I mouthed "thanks," and reached into my own pocket. "Abby, your dad saved you," I said. "But he didn't make it all the way across himself, understand? We could see him go around the bend. They're looking for him now."

"Get back to work, you can't just walk off!" I heard Father shouting to all his hired crew who were now finding their way down stream looking for Jim Ross. They disappeared around the point. It wasn't very long before they returned. One of them stepped over to where we were still sitting.

"Did you find him?" Abby asked between her sobs.

"We did," he said. "But the river got him." He then took Amos aside. I could barely make out what they were saying.

"Where?" Amos asked.

"Floating in the edge of the eddy where we tied up the boats."

"Okay, make a woods stretcher, a camp blanket wrapped around two poles. Hike across to that hunting camp on the rise over there, see?" Amos was pointing to an old camp, nearly indistinguishable from the green mossy fir trees towering all around it. "It's our family's hunting camp. The door is always unlocked. Go inside and you'll find some wool blankets in a wooden chest. Use those to wrap him in and to make the stretcher so we can get him in the boat. See if there's some rope, too." When we got to the boats, there was Jim Ross, wrapped up in a green army wool blanket on a "woods stretcher" that was supported by a couple of boards set across the thwarts of the bateau. This was Jim's last boat ride.

Rowing back to the depot at Black Pond was a blur. Father stayed to direct the rest of the men. The crew seemed a little spooked as they guided logs down the river channel to the waiting boom. Abby sobbed quietly as she sat by her father's body. Uncle Amos and I rowed the Maynard bateau from the eddy across Black Pond. Abby sat on the front seat, facing the stern. Uncle Amos and I rowed, and with four oars in the water, we made good time.

It wasn't an easy job managing the oars. The long logs we had just rolled into the river now floated down with the current all around us. There was nowhere to put an oar in, logs floating everywhere side to side, end to end. We shipped our oars and started to pole our way through a river now clogged with our winter's work. I was praying a sudden wind wouldn't jam them into us. It could crush the boat like ice floes in the Arctic. When we reached the larger logs holding everything back, we had to find the trip log, the one skinny enough to slide the Maynard bateau over.

Rose and Olive were at the door with Erik and Bear. They knew something had happened seeing two boats returning, not anywhere near quitting time. Uncle Amos was the one to tell Rose and Olive. Abby climbed out of the boat and went to her aunt, both in tears now. Olive guided them into the cabin while Uncle Amos and I set the stretcher into a far corner of *The Twilight* that rested peacefully along the crude dock. Amos took Bear, Erik, Rose, Abby and me back to the Katahdin Inn. Jim's body rode undisturbed on *The Twilight*'s rear deck. Word had spread. There were people everywhere along the breakwater and down to the Village dock when we motored in. Louis, who had remained in the village, was the first person to help tie up the boat.

Rose was watching from above the breakwater, handkerchief to her face, quietly sobbing. Olive and Erik were beside her. I saw Olive put her arm over Rose's shoulders; she seemed inconsolable. Bear trotted down to the dock to greet us, tail wagging at first, but as he got closer, the tail dropped, his ears went back and he sniffed at the green bundle that had been his best friend.

Uncle Amos and I dug out a coffin stored in the barn. We had a few left over after we stopped using coffins to ship *Tanglefoot*. I helped load the long pine box into a wagon and then drove it down to *The Twilight*. It took all our strength to move Jim into the coffin. Uncle Amos looked down at the blanket wrapped body, his hand resting on the coffin's side.

"Well, Jim, it's time to say goodbye. I hope you have a good last run down the river." And with those words, Uncle Amos set and nailed the lid while I held it in place. I sat down on a crate when he was finished, my head in my hands. I wasn't feeling so good.

"You okay, Charlie?" Uncle Amos asked.

"Not really. I was just thinking about Mother and Tommy." I wiped away a tear. "I keep thinking that you and I could be nailing this lid over Abby after that crazy ride down the Devil's Staircase."

"If you worry about what you could lose, you'll worry all the time," he said.

"She could have been killed," I said. "And not just from going off the road then, but getting rolled over by saw logs." It was difficult to accept the fact that Abby was not a cautious person.

The horse hauled the wagon into the barn. It was a safe place to leave Jim in his coffin until the last ride to the cemetery. I unhitched Duke, put him in his stall and went back with Uncle Amos to finish the drive at Black Pond.

Driving Boots
Chapter 7

The morning before the funeral, boat loads of rivermen started to arrive. Several rode horses over the Deer Pond Road. There wasn't a spare bed to be had in the Village. Several tents had sprouted in the hay field next to the Inn. Hiram and I were in the Pleasant Hill Cemetery digging Jim's final resting place early in the morning of the graveside service. His driving boots would soon be hanging from a tree on the river bank where he was last seen.

"His time came early," I said.

"It did." We were at the awkward stage in grave digging when two diggers would get in each other's way. Hiram stepped aside and gave me the room….and the work.

"The Stone People seemed to live forever. Hand me that spade, please."

I grabbed the short shovel with the grab handle and handed it to Hiram, then I got out of his way. Dirt flew like he was an industrious wood-chuck. After ten minutes, he handed the shovel to me.

"Who were they?"

"They came from the frozen north. When they got to a village, they would kill and eat everyone they could find, then burn the village and hunt those who they thought had gotten away."

"Cannibals?"

"With an insatiable appetite, but they died out a very long time ago."

"How could they have died out with so many villages near them?"

"The legend tells of a group of hunters who sealed the entire tribe of Stone People in a cave," Hiram said.

"I sure wouldn't want to meet up with those hunters," I said.

"Me neither. See if you can help me get this rock out of here," Hiram said. We tussled with the large rock, rolling it on a plank out of the grave and into the woods.

"Found your spot yet, Charlie?" Hiram asked. "Your special place?"

"Nope. Still looking, but nothing yet," I replied.

"You know, it'll probably be where you least expect it," he observed.

"I keep looking, but it hasn't shown up yet." My special place was just that. Every person has one, according to Hiram, and I'd know it if I found it. How I'd know exactly, I have no idea, but I was supposed to 'feel it.' It might be sitting on a rock on shore, or it could be a chopping block by the woodshed. Wherever it was, it was supposed to give me an opportunity for reflection and calm.

In another hour we had the grave finished and went back to the lodge to clean up before the service.

While I was washing my hands, the bible salesman walked into the kitchen, empty coffee mug in hand.

"The pot is on the stove behind me," I said.

"Thanks," he said as he walked to the stove to pour a cup. "I've got some great things to show you, my friend," he said. "Just give me a minute to get my case. I'd given up finding you!" He put down the still empty mug and headed for the hallway. In a moment he returned with his sample case which he slid onto the table, waving an invitation to come check out his bible store as he popped the case open. I sighed to myself. The last thing I wanted in my life was another bible. Mine was lost in the fire along with Mother who had given it to me a few years ago. In the case I could see two bibles, an assortment of prayer shawls, rosary beads and crosses. Then I saw the gold painted cross, encrusted with multi-colored glass jewels top to bottom, and I thought, That's perfect!!

....

We had been full at the Inn the last two days. Woodsmen from all over came to say goodbye to Jim Ross, possibly the best-known river driver in the country. There were no more seats in the church when the service began. At least a dozen men, hats in hand, stood outside serenading us with logging ballads. The casket was closed, a simple unfinished pine box with rope handles on the sides. Uncle Amos had carved a pine tree on the lid. Flowers were sent all the way from Bangor. The new minister, now wearing shoes that Olive found for him and a jacket Rose dug out of Jim's closet, was approaching the lectern. He had left his sample case in the Inn, but had done a pretty good business selling bibles, hymnals, crosses and the like.

Rose and Abby sat in the front row between me and Uncle Amos. Father was late coming back with a crew, but walked in the door just before the service started. He joined us in front, taking a seat beside Uncle Amos. Outside, the group of men singing logging songs with a fiddler and a man playing the mouth harp had finished their ballad and were now quiet.

"Everything okay?" I heard Uncle Amos ask as Father slid into a chair beside him.

"As good as it's going to be," Father said, glancing over his shoulder at the door as if something had followed him.

"What?" Uncle Amos asked. Father shook his head as if to say, not now. The minister came to the lectern where he placed some papers he had taken from the inside pocket of the borrowed suit-coat.

"We're gathered here today to pay our respects to the greatest riverman of them all, Jim Ross." Abby squeezed my hand. A tear fell down her cheek. "Jim was well known coast to coast. He knew more about how to get a pine log from the river bank to the sawmill than anyone else." There was more praise as several in the gathering came up to share their remembrances. One told the story of when Jim found a live black tailed wasp's nest hanging from a rafter in his cabin. He tore the grey football sized nest off the rafter and stuffed it in his already-burning wood stove before the wasps could figure out what was happening. After a few minutes, he opened the door to add a log, but instead of a puff of grey smoke, a black cloud of angry survivors flew out into the cabin. There were a few more laughs.

The room got quiet as the minister turned to look at Abby. It looked like he was going to ask her if she wanted to say anything. But Abby sat still, quietly wiping tears from her face, not looking up. The moment passed. The minister gave a closing prayer and asked that the family exit the building first so others could express condolences on their way out.

It was a nice service. We followed the horse drawn wagon up the hill to the cemetery with Jim's coffin bouncing in back. Right behind it were Rose and Abby, then the rest of us. We stood around one side of the grave, fanned out around the minister. Bear sat down beside Abby, not seeming to mind the leash. The coffin was lowered, words were said, tears were dried and we walked back to the Inn where there was food and drink for everyone. Folks were in groups here and there, talking about escapades, real or imagined, that they had had with Jim Ross. Hiram stayed to fill in the grave.

"Charlie, we need more ice." Olive was freshening up the punch bowl that had more *Tanglefoot* in it than punch. I grabbed the ice tongs hanging on the wall in the back shed and pulled the ice house door open. With the block of ice firmly in the tongs, I swung it over my shoulder for the short trip back. Just outside the back door were two rivermen sitting on the wood pile and playing a game of cards. I hadn't seen them on my way out.

"If you ask me, it's the girl's fault," one said.

"She never should have come up there," said the other. "Jim wouldn't have had to rescue her, and he'd still be with us. Women are bad luck on a river drive."

I walked past them with the block of ice in tongs over my shoulder. They seemed too busy with the card game to pay attention to me. I dropped the block of ice into the wash tub and went at it with the pick, then transferred ice chips to a bowl to refresh the punch.
Father was in a serious conversation with Mr. Martin. Abby was placing a tray of sandwiches on the table. I went over to help make room for it.

"I don't think any of the river drivers like me very much," she whispered to me. "Some think it's my fault he died."

"I just heard two of them talking about that," I said.

I grabbed Abby's arm and walked her out of the room to a quiet corner of the porch. Bear Dog followed us, his waving tail nearly knocking a teacup off a table.

"How was that your fault?" I asked her.

"If I hadn't been there, he'd still be alive," she said, a tear finding its way down her cheek. She wiped it away.

"He could still have been hit by that log whether you were there or not, just not under the same circumstances," I pointed out. "The accident had nothing to do with you." Abby and I had a better understanding of consequences, intended or not, than most. Our trip to Grandmother Molly's a month ago made that clear. When we brought Little Rabbit back with us, an entire family disappeared because she had left the timestream she belonged in.

"He could have been, Charlie, but he wasn't. He gave his life saving mine. It's pretty simple," she observed. "I'm kind of okay with that because I know he loved me a lot, but it doesn't make things any easier without him anymore."

"We should go in. Folks are going to want to offer their condolences."

"Yeah, but not everyone, apparently."

We walked back inside, letting Bear play with Heidrick. Abby was summoned by Rose who was talking with Mr. Martin. I walked out toward the main veranda.

"So, what's going on?" I heard Uncle Amos ask Father. I paused at the doorway to the porch right behind their chairs.

"The gun smuggling arrangement is off. Feds are crawling all over the delivery route, so that's shut down for now. We have a new order for *Tanglefoot* from Martin, and a big one, too, so you'll be busy enough soon." Father looked outside at Bear, sitting quietly beside Heidrick. "Rose say anything about Jim's dog?"

"She said that she and Abby were talking about him and thought Bear might be happier being here with Abby." Uncle Amos took out his can of Virginia Dare cut tobacco, poured some into a pipe bowl, and struck a match. "When are the logs coming down?"

"They should be in the boom at the mouth of Caucmagomic by tomorrow night. We'll hire one of the tow boats to get them down the lake." Father took a long pull of a flask he kept in his vest. "You really outdid yourself with this batch, Amos," Father said smiling as he lifted his flask in a rare tribute to his brother.

"The secret is in the casks. Oak is the best for creating that smooth finish," he said. "The good stuff takes seven years to age properly. We have only seven days between filling the barrel and delivery."

"Would it make more sense to sell more barrels and fewer bottles?" Father asked.

"That would be easiest in packaging, but hardest in hiding and moving. Besides, it could take longer. A case of bottles will go under hay or a manure pile a lot easier and a lot faster than a forty-gallon oak cask. Cussed things weigh over three hundred pounds," Amos took another sip of lightning.

Abby had escaped to the lawn where she was rubbing Bear's belly. I went out to join her.

"He's a good dog," I said. "I'm glad you have him. Just look at how calm he is while you're doing that!" Bear's head was back, and

Abby was stroking the underneath of his chin and throat.

"Calm now, but just wait until he sees one of the rabbits living under those old lilac bushes." Abby looked up at me. "I think we should talk with Hiram," she said.

"About seeing Moosis?"

"That isn't the only thing. Do you remember when we passed over the site of *The Tethys'* wreck?" She asked.

"I do. You seemed like you'd seen a ghost."

"I did, kind of. Not just one, either. I could sense every fear and every emotion those thirty-four men felt while the boat burned and they shivered on the stumps, wondering where their buddies were and how long they had before they froze to death. I'd never felt that way before," she said. "And then yesterday, I walked by the old Strickland farm and could sense what happened there when the old man went nuts and shot his family, then himself. I don't know why I'm sensing these things now. It's been going on ever since we saw Moosis on the Devil's Staircase."

We sat in silence. Bear nuzzled my arm, looking for a pat.

"We should ask Hiram about seeing Moosis, too." I scratched Bear behind his ears.

Hiram was my mentor. His Wabanaki ancestry was evident throughout his little cabin, set between giant pines overlooking the lake. Dreamcatchers hung from the porch roof. A bear skin adorned one wall, and moose horns were above his doorway. Hiram knew the old legends and the old ways.

"Olive needs some help cleaning up. Want to join me?" Abby took my outstretched hand and I helped her stand up. After a quick hug, I asked, "You doing okay?"

"Sometimes, sometimes not," she said.
"I know what you mean," I said. We held hands as we walked back inside. Guests came and went, and a few offered their condolences to Abby.

Weasel Tail
Chapter 8

The next morning, we were off to Hiram's. His cabin was a short hike to the lower village. We had to walk by the site of my first home, the village hotel that burned a few years ago, taking Mother and my friend, Tommy, from us. The cellar hole had been filled in and the rest of the yard turned into a potato field. As we passed by, Abby stopped, staring at the site.

"What's going on?" I asked, stopping beside her. Her shoulders were trembling. Abby didn't respond right away.

"It was very fast," she said.

"What was fast?"

"When they died. They just went to sleep from the smoke."

"How could you know?" I asked. I had never spoken about the specific details of their last moments alive. My heart ached so whenever I thought of it. I think I just hadn't wanted to know what it must have been like.

"I can see it, Charlie." She wiped her hand across the side of her face. "I'm not feeling so hot." Abby ducked behind the giant white birch tree beside the village lane as if she were going to be sick. I followed around to see if I could help, at least hold back her beautiful red hair.

What I saw is hard to describe. Abby was there, but she wasn't. She was fading as she walked away from me toward the new potato field. I could see some of the forest and distant buildings through her. When she turned and walked back in my direction, she became solid again.

"Abby? Are you okay? What's going on? I watched you fade

away!"

"The paths," she said, staring at the new potato field.

"Paths?"

"They're like threads of gold, snaking through the woods. There are so many! I started to follow one, but I was afraid I might not find my way back." Abby was still trembling. I put my hand on her shoulder to reassure her, and she seemed to relax. "What's going on, Charlie?"

"I don't see anything. Where are you looking?"

"Over there," she pointed. I still couldn't see anything like she was describing. "What do you think would happen if I walked along one of those golden paths?" she wondered aloud.

"Let's find out. Hiram will know," I assured her, taking her hand in mine and resuming our walk to Hiram's cabin. Abby slipped back into a trance as we walked, unaware of her surroundings. She was quiet for the rest of the walk to Hiram's.

Hiram heard us walking up his grassy path and greeted us with a shout before we even got to the clearing just below the cabin. His hearing was unusually sharp. We walked onto the front porch. Hiram was standing in the doorway, a hand carved figurine of a bear in one hand and a carving knife in the other.

"You okay, Abby?" he asked her before banging the screen door a couple of times to push the skeeters away before inviting us inside. "You look like you've seen a ghost!" he exclaimed, placing the totem and his carving knife on the table. "Here," he motioned to a chair beside the kitchen table. "You should sit." He took Abby's arm and led her to the chair. Abby seemed distracted and almost unaware of her surroundings.

"What's happened?" he asked. Abby just sat there. Hiram looked at me when she didn't respond.

"Abby and I were walking by our old place," I said. Hiram turned from me and looked at her. "I don't know how else to say this, but she started to disappear."

"Abby," Hiram said, a little louder. She gave no response. "Abby, it's Hiram and Charlie," he said, and then reached out to her. The moment he placed his hand on her shoulder, she turned to him with a little jump, disoriented, as if waking from a nightmare.

"Hi, Hiram," she said with some hesitation, looking around the cabin as if suddenly realizing where she was. "What happened? How did I get here?" She wiped her hand across her face again, shaking the cobwebs from her dark thoughts as she smoothed her hair.

"We walked here by the old hotel," I told her. "You said you felt

funny and then started to disappear. You've been in a daze ever since."
She began to come out of it.

"It was the oddest sensation," she said. "I could see the old hotel in flames, and I was looking right into the room where your mother and Tommy perished. I could look through the upstairs window. The room they were in was filling with smoke. There was nothing I could do."

"Did you see anything else?" asked Hiram, head cocked to one side.

"I wasn't feeling very well and thought I was going to throw up, so I leaned against the big white birch. When I felt a little better, I looked up to see several golden paths crisscrossing where the hotel used to be," she explained. "They were really pretty, the paths dappled in golden sunlight, and they all seemed so inviting. I could see a distance down one and took a few steps. It was weird. Almost at once, the Village seemed to disappear. It scared me, so I stepped back."

"When did this start?" Hiram asked. From the table, he picked up the block of wood he had been carving when we walked inside.

"The day after we saw Moosis on the Devil's Staircase," she said. "We were going to the Cuxabexis Depot. I knew it when we passed over the site of the boat explosion. I could hear the screams from the dying men. It was awful."

On a cold, late November afternoon three years ago, Father's boat caught fire while ferrying immigrant woods workers and supplies to a depot in back of Gero Island. The engine caught fire, there was an explosion, and seventeen men died. It had taken two days to find all but one of them. That last body showed up the next May. I know all about those screams. I was there.

"Tell me more about when you saw Moosis," Hiram asked.

"We saw Moosis' spirit on the Devil's Staircase after we ran off the road," Abby described. Hiram stopped whittling, folded his pocket knife and slipped it into his jeans. He placed the wooden bear totem he had been carving on the little table beside him.

"How did he appear?" Hiram didn't look surprised.

"His face was painted as if he was going to war. He looked really fierce and carried a spear decorated with feathers," I said. "On his back was a bow, a quiver and arrows."

"You could have been killed there," Hiram said.

"No kidding," said Abby. "Now we check the brakes before we leave the yard."

"Maybe that's why Moosis appeared," Hiram explained.

"Because we were in danger?" I asked.

"You nearly died running booze," Hiram said. "In a brakeless run down a moonlit descent of the Devil's Staircase."

"He beckoned us to come with him," Abby said. "I think it's something more than protecting us here and now, if that's what you're getting at."

"Maybe he needs your help," Hiram suggested. "The bigger question is should you go back to find out why?"

"We went to the old aerie," I said.

"What, here, now?" a surprised Hiram asked. We went there on our trip to Grandmother Molly's original village, and Hiram was wondering if we had time-traveled again.

"Here," Abby said, "and now. On the other side of Caucmagomic Mountain by the caves.

"I wanted to see where 'Ki'kwa'jenu used to live," I said. "I've seen his red eyes glowing between the tops of the pines on Caucmagomic Ridge, and his black wings are often following me at a distance."

"What did you find?" he asked.

"Part of a necklace and several broken spear points," I reported. "I think there was a fight there with more than one brave."

"Did you move them?" Hiram asked.

"No, we thought it best to leave the beads where they were," Abby said.

"And we saw Moosis again," I said.

"How did he appear?" Hiram asked, one eyebrow raised.

"He came really close to us," said Abby. "He was wearing war paint and held a spear in his hand just like the first time."

"The point looked just like the one he gave me the last time we saw each other," I added.

"I wonder what he wanted," Hiram said. "Spirits don't show up unless there's a good reason."

Hiram picked up his pipe. "Are there any other places where you sense the past?" Hiram asked. He stuffed the briar bowl with Virginia Dare, the Village's favorite tobacco, and struck a match on the arm of his chair.

"Once when Charlie and I were walking across the old mud flats. Where the old places used to be before Rip Dam was built? When the water went down last fall, we did some exploring. I had a strong sense that something was wrong, almost a cry for help from where the old homes used to be. Just a pile of stone and brick now. And then there's the old Strickland Farm that burned, but nothing as clear as what just happened by the old hotel." Abby looked at Hiram. "What's going on?"

"Mrs. Strickland was trapped on the top floor of the house after the lightning strike killed her husband in the barn and set both ablaze." Hiram paused. "I've heard about two others in the Otter Clan like you. And that's over a long period of time, too. Maybe there's one only every century," he explained.

"One what?" I asked.

He turned to Abby as if to study her face. "Pathfinder," Hiram replied. "Some say a 'Deep-Seeing One.' That may be your special power. If the tribe were lucky enough to have a member who was a Pathfinder, they'd know the best place to make camp, where the best water was, where to cross the river, and where the best hunting and fishing could be found. Besides all that, the Pathfinder knew all the things that happened anywhere, in any field, or in any hut. Whether she wanted to or not."

"Is this something I can turn on or off at will?" Abby asked.

Hiram thought a second before replying. "It will take some work to understand this power," he said. "You will be more sensitive to what's happened at any place, and it's my guess that you will be able to tune it out or pay attention to it at will, but that takes time and practice."

"But what about the golden paths I saw at the old hotel?" Abby asked.

"There are great risks following one of those," Hiram warned.

"Like disappearing?" I wondered.

"Time passes differently along those golden paths. While following one, it might take a few minutes. While following it, that same journey would seem longer to those not following. There's no way to know. You disappear from here and show up at a different place and at a different time. The greatest problem is finding your way back to the same place you started from in the timestream." It sounded risky, I thought.

"Just before we left for home, Moosis gave me a spear point. Maybe he wants me to return it?" I wondered.

"Where's the spear point now?" Hiram asked.

"I buried it at the point before we left Grey Wolf's village. I thought it would be fun to find it so many centuries later. I didn't think it was terribly valuable."

"You have to find it, Charlie," Abby said. "It could be really important."

"I know that now. We should do it today," I replied.

"What did Moosis' spirit do after he revealed himself?" Hiram asked.

"He guided us to the chimney that leads to the nest," I explained.

"How many times have you seen the Nighthawk?" Hiram asked.

I sighed. "A few times," I said. "It's coming out at all times of day and night, and seems to be larger as it gets closer. Then it disappears. One morning, just before sunrise, I could see its eyes glowing on the ridge. This beast is so much larger than ordinary hawks."

"Ki'kwa'jenu was a huge monster in the beginning," Hiram explained. "He was a true raptor with razor sharp talons and a beak that could break large bones. He guarded his territory just like Pomola did on the opposite side of the great mountain. He was stronger then, too. His descendants are small hawks, and only mice and squirrels fear it." Hiram knew all the old tales. "Besides its young, the tribes believed it guarded a treasure in the mountains. You know how ravens like collecting shiny jewels to adorn their nests. Ki'kwa'jenu was no different. If someone was foolish enough to look for it, they rarely returned. And the few treasure-seekers who did escape the razor-sharp talons of that huge beast left their minds behind. All became insane."

"I can understand that," I said. "Ki'kwa'jenu is driving me nuts! How does it get here?"

"It may have found one of the ancient trails." He puffed on his pipe. There was something calming about the smell of the tobacco, as sweet as cedar smoke.

"Can anyone follow a Pathfinder?" I asked.

"Yes, anyone could follow right behind them, as close as its shadow but never out of sight. The trails are interwoven, like giant spider webs. It would be an easy thing to take a wrong turn and get lost forever. Pathfinders have great power." Hiram explained. "They would always find their way back home. It just might not be in the same timestream as when they left."

"I wonder if that's how Moosis showed up," I wondered out loud.

"Spirits have their own ways to travel," Hiram said, "using pathways through the heavens. It often takes the skill of a shaman to make that journey."

When Hiram said that, I understood the danger I might be in. Ki'kwa'jenu was allied with Kabibonokka, the north wind of destruction. It seemed to covet my power of the South Wind, Sowanakik. Were both after me? Did the north wind push the air under the Nighthawk's black wings?

"The Nighthawk has followed you through time. It has to be destroyed," Hiram said, "or you'll never be free of it."

"Maybe that's what Moosis wants to tell me. Could he want us to help him take care of Ki'kwa'jenu for good?" I turned to Abby. "We have to go back, don't we?"

"I'm sure of it," she said. "We should get to Grandmother Molly's soon."

"There is a story you should hear before you go," Hiram said. "Once there was a hunter named Weasel Tail. He was a Pathfinder like you, Abby. He had just grown into a man and was just getting used to his special skill. He knew where the game was and told the hunting parties where they'd have success. He was so popular that he married the chief's most beautiful daughter who brought many furs into their new wigwam. In his hunting travels, Weasel Tail had taken some of these special paths, but there was nothing very different at the end of each one. He would turn around and come right home. Everything seemed to be the same when he returned."

"I've always worried about things not being quite the same as when we left," Charlie said.

"Maybe Weasel Tail worried about that, too," Abby turned to Hiram. "What happened to him?"

Hiram continued. "One day, he saw a path he had somehow missed. It looked perfect, snaking across the mountain as the sun rose behind the mist that often covered Pomola's hunting grounds. He decided to follow it. There was nothing different at the end, only more mountain and more mist. He didn't think he had been gone very long, but when he returned to his village, it was no longer there. The remains of what had been his longhouse was collapsed on the ground, rotting away under the leaves. The other huts had been taken down long before he arrived. Weasel Tail didn't know what had happened, so he asked Wise Owl, who was perched in a nearby birch tree. 'Oh, they've been gone a long, long time,' Wise Owl said.

"'How long?' Weasel Tail asked.

"'Years and years. Most have traveled to live with the spirits of Katahdin. The rest moved to the village down the valley,' and Wise Owl flew away.

"When Weasel Tail got to the village farther down the valley, he learned he had been away fifty summers. None of his family was alive.

No one knew him, he didn't recognize anyone, and was truly alone. So be careful if you find one of these trails and decide to follow it."

"You're saying that if I follow one of those paths, I could return fifty years later?" Abby asked.

"That could happen. Being a Pathfinder has much risk," Hiram added.

"I want to go to Grandmother Molly's right away," Abby said. Grandmother Molly lived in a village in Nicatou, where the East Branch joins the West Branch of the Penobscot River. She was the village's healer but held a secret that only Abby, Hiram and I knew. Grandmother Molly was a time-traveler whose father, Grey Wolf, sent her to our time for her own protection. The thirty-five-hundred-year trip was managed by using a special amulet she had bestowed on Abby and used in a special place. When we first met Grandmother Molly, she sent us back to her homeland to collect plants needed to cure an illness in her village.

"We should get to Nicatou. I know Awasosqua will have more to say about this. I'll join you there. I know it's been only weeks since I last saw her, but I really miss that old bear." Awasosqua was Grandmother Molly's name when she lived here before her father, Grey Wolf, sent her to our time to protect her and the amulet.

"Otter clan, right?" I asked.

"One of thirteen clans," Hiram said. "There are thirteen rocks set around the fire pit in the sweat lodge, and thirteen scales on Turtle's back." he added. He looked us over and smiled as if he knew how everything would play out. "I think a sweat lodge is in your future."

"When?" asked Abby. She seemed eager.

"When we have a celebration to welcome the Pathfinder into the Otter Clan." He lit his pipe and smooshed a mosquito on the window pane. "Soon, then?"

"As soon as we can pack!" I said.

We thanked him for his help and began the walk home. We went down Hiram's trail to the Village road and started back to the Inn. We were quiet for a while. I was thinking what might happen if Abby saw another path. She would have to explore where and when it led. She was an explorer. I don't think I would take that risk.

The A.B. Smith was towing a boom of logs down the lake. The wind had come up from the south, and whitecaps were starting to take shape. Soon, swells would appear as the waves got organized. We stopped to watch.

"They have about an hour to anchor that boom," I said. "Then, the wind will beach it on the ledges."

"The tow boat won't make much headway in the wind," Abby said.

"You're right. The waves will roll the pulpwood out from under the boom log necklace. A lot of wood could get washed out of the boom, there's increased pressure on the chains and logs, and something is apt to break. Then, there'll be a big mess to clean up." We were standing on a ledge on the shore of the lake. The wind had pushed the boom so close to shore that we could have hit it with a rock. An eye-hook with a thick iron ring passing through it was set deep into the highest part of the ledge. Lead had been poured around it and then pounded in to jam the iron pin and ring firmly in the hole.

"Katahdin looks big today," Abby said. "I can see Pomola Peak pretty well. Isn't there a story about Ki'kwa'jenu and the north wind? I think it took place around there."

"There is," I said. "The Nighthawk joined up with the north wind, Kabibonokka. Whenever Ki'kwa'jenu wanted to go out hunting for dinner, the north wind was supposed to blow to keep its prey from smelling it. The hungrier the Nighthawk was, the stronger the wind needed to be. One day, the north wind blew so hard, all the water in the lakes disappeared and much of the forest was flattened. Fish died. Creatures were dying from thirst. When Katahdin found out, he put a stop to it. No deals could be made with the winds, but wind spirits may still choose to inhabit certain persons."

"Certain persons like you, right?" She smiled.

"Yeah, like me." I smiled back. "Do you remember the night *The Tethys* blew up?"

"I remember hearing about it, but you haven't said very much,"

"I don't like to think about it. When *The Tethys* blew up, I was thrown off the bow into the icy water. Part of a cast iron cook stove pinned me to the bottom. I couldn't get free."

"But how did you get out?" she asked.

"When I looked to the surface, I could see black wings outlined by orange-red flames. The Nighthawk's wings were headed right for me. I thought it was all over."

"So how did you get free?" she asked again.

"It was Father. He was the black wings that night. He pulled me out from under the stove." I looked away.

"But he's not really, right? Ki'kwa'jenu has nothing to do with him, right?" Abby asked, hope in her voice.

"I sometimes wonder," I said.

....

The next morning Abby and I paddled a canoe up Caucmagomic Stream to the site of the accident. Abby had a pair of her father's caulked boots. I had brought a shovel. I helped her hang Jim's driving boots from a stout branch of a pine that hung over the river bank where he had disappeared into the Penobscot River watershed and eternity.

We had a quiet paddle back. Halfway over to the Village, we took a break and drifted. The air was so clear and the mountain range seemed much larger. The hot sun gave the newly varnished canoe a familiar smell. We floated across the mirrored lake, ripples from the canoe making the reflection of Mt. Katahdin dance. Soon, we pulled the canoe onto the sandy shore where an old saw log had washed up. The mark stamped on the end indicated that it had come from north of the Village. Abby hopped out and steadied the canoe while Bear and I stepped ashore.

"Let's sit a minute," I said. We relaxed on the log. Bear was beside Abby.

"This is where I want to be, Charlie." Abby took a deep breath. We were sitting on the shore of Graveyard Point just beyond the Inn. Katahdin was so clear, it seemed one could reach out and touch it. "I can't think of a nicer place to live." Bear nuzzled his nose against her neck, licking her ear in approval.

"My mother is here," I said, "and both your parents." I put my arm around Abby. Abby's mother had died from childbirth fever after Abby's brother was born. Her infant brother did not survive. Both were in the same grave. "You know you're pretty special to me," I said, looking at her. I gave her hand a squeeze.

"Thanks, Charlie. It's not easy to put some feelings into words." She looked at me. "But we won't be in the moonshine business forever, right?" Abby turned to me. "Prohibition isn't going to last."

"No, it probably won't." I laughed. I took the shovel. We walked up to the shoreline of trees.

"I feel Dad is looking over us. He hung up more than one pair of caulked boots by the rivers both here and in Oregon. He never thought his boots would be dangling from a tree branch leaning over the river bank."

"Knowing he died doing what he loved doesn't make things any easier," I said.

"No, it sure doesn't." I saw Abby turn to look at Mt. Katahdin.

"His spirit is roaming with Pomola and Wichowen," she said. "I'm so glad it happened here and not far away in Oregon." Abby sighed and turned back to me. "Aren't you curious about finding the spear point Moosis gave you?"

"You bet," I said. We could see the Inn through the trees. We walked up to a large rock beside which I had buried the point. Not much of the rock was above ground now. There was a US Geological Survey plate set into the top. I paced off the number of steps I remembered and started digging where I thought I would find the spear point. I dug forever. Paced, dug. Paced, dug. First one hole, then another, then connecting them.

"This isn't working, Abby." I said. "It's not where I buried it!"

"Oh, and just who came along, dug it up, and made off with it? Huh? I swear, Charlie, sometimes…." She was shaking her head in dismay. "I think you'll find it over there," she said. "I can feel it."

"Feel it?" I asked.

"Yes, it's weird, I know," she replied. I went back to digging and measuring. I understood shovels better than spear point migration, apparently. In my frustration, I was flinging dirt all over.

"No, Charlie, move over a foot," she directed. So I did. When I had gone about a foot down, Abby shouted. Bear jumped.

"There it is, Charlie, you just found it!" She ran to the mountain of dirt. There on the side was the spear point still in perfect condition, although a bit dirty. I had never seen it in the hole and must have piled on at least two more shovelfuls of dirt on top of it after I heaved it up.

I took the stone down to the lake and washed off some of the dirt. It was a beautiful point, a red jasper chert with mostly gold colored veins that cut across from side to side. There were also a few veins of dark green, cream yellow and jet black I hadn't paid much attention to when I first held it. And when I raised it to the sun, the light shone through as if the veins themselves were telling me how special a stone this was. I could almost hear the stone speaking to me. I handed the point to Abby.

"I wonder why Moosis gave this to you," she asked, handing it back.

"He must have had a good reason," I said. "Moosis will tell us more when we get back to Grey Wolf's village." Bear began whining.

"Close to dinner, Bear?" Abby asked. Bear wagged his tail in expectation. That was a hint that we needed to hurry back to the Inn to help with dinner.

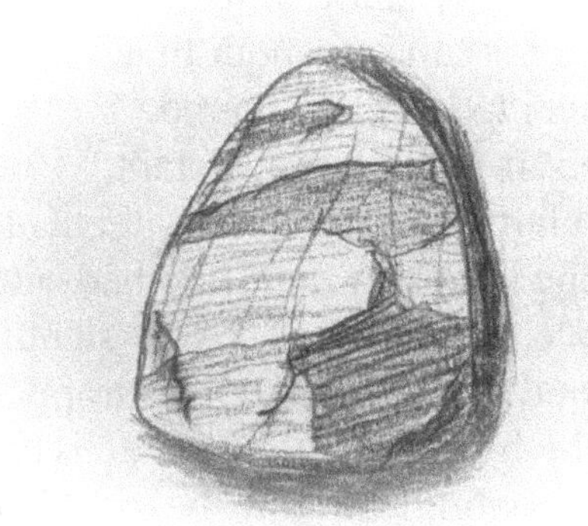

The Nighthawk Distillery
Chapter 9

"We have to go back. Something's wrong," Abby said. She didn't mean back to Grandmother Molly's village, but to Grey Wolf's village in a different timestream. It seemed to be the only way to find out why Moosis was appearing to us. The amulet Grandmother Molly gave to Abby had powers that, with the right words in the right place, the speaker and everything she was touching traveled back in time.

"We'll have to be careful about the consequences," I said. "It's really risky, Abby."

It was after dinner, and we sat quietly on a log still waiting on shore to be rolled into the cove's boom. "I need to talk with Father," I said.

"About?" she asked.

"About money. I'm old enough for a share of the profits, a fair share, and you haven't seen any money, right?"

"Right," she confirmed. "Nothing yet."

"That has to change," I said. We followed the noise of hammering that came from the forge.

We found them in the barn. Uncle Amos was making some drift pins. Father was ranting about something, pacing back and forth as Uncle Amos turned his urge to pound Father into hammering white-hot steel bars to make drift pins for pier building instead. I wanted Uncle Amos to be a mediator between me and Father if it came to that. I did know that I was telling him that Abby and I were taking a week off. I wasn't asking. We were leaving in the morning.

I started by telling Father that it was past time for a serious conversation about the family business and my share in it.

"Great constipated Christ! We're not talking about that." Father handed Uncle Amos another piece of steel to heat and pound.

"You should listen to him, Caleb. It could be important," Uncle Amos said. Father's cigar was firmly clamped between his teeth. His eyes pivoted to Uncle Amos, then snapped back to me. If he had bitten the cigar stub any harder, he would have cut it in half. I was standing between him and the door and Abby stood beside me. He was trapped.

"Abby and I want our share of the business after each delivery," I began. "Anyone else working for you would have to be paid." He looked me over as if sizing up my determination.

"I don't know, Charlie," Father said, tearing the cigar butt out from his teeth, throwing it out the barn door. "There are a lot of expenses, expenses you don't know about." The veins in his temples were getting more pronounced, but his face wasn't very red just yet. That told me he was considering what was being said to him rather than rejecting it entirely.

"And there is a lot coming in, too," I countered. "And I do know about that. We're family, and loyal to the business and I thought loyal to each other. Don't we deserve our fair share? You pay the county sheriff and a judge every trip out. Why not us?"

"He has a point, Caleb," Amos said. "We couldn't run the business without these two. Anyone else we'd have to hire, and they'd probably be wagging their tongues all over the county." There was silence. Father's eyes bulged toward Amos, then to Abby and finally to me. He let out a big sigh and then seemed to relax. We had him.

"Tell me, Charlie. What should we do about Mr. Martin?" Father was testing me.

"You've said nothing about your arrangements with him," I replied. "But I don't trust him, and I think he's building an inventory to undersell us."

"He wants nearly the entire production of the stills," Uncle Amos explained. "That wouldn't leave much for the rest of our customers."

"There are three more stills waiting to be set up, right?" I asked.

"In the back of the barn," Caleb replied. "We don't have enough mash yet."

"I'd set them up in a different location and get those supplies," I suggested. "If we don't make that a priority, we'll have lost our smaller, steadier customers as we divert the still's output to Martin."

"It's more complicated than that," Caleb said. "There's a cost to make that happen."

"Then we have to spend the money," Uncle Amos said. "If we don't, the payments from Martin won't be enough to cover our costs." Father was pretty tight with a dollar. "After the last deal we made, prices for all the raw materials have increased, and you just told me that the sheriff isn't the only one wanting more pay-off."

"How would you deal with the Boston gang?" Father asked me.

"We supply them like anyone else," Abby broke in. "They get a special price to encourage them to leave us alone, and we add security to our deliveries. We don't run guns, no matter what they say."

"Take a firm stand?" Father asked. "The consequences could be serious."

"Not if we protect ourselves, on the delivery route, here, and at the delivery site," Abby replied. "There are plenty of Bangor Tigers looking for some work." Father seemed to be thinking things over.

"Alright," Father conceded. He seemed almost relieved, and I think he had been expecting this conversation to take place at some point because it was almost too easy.

"What's your proposal?" he asked.

"Let's plan a quarter share for the business," I replied. That money will repair and replace, possibly expand the distillery."

"What about the rest?" Uncle Amos asked.

"The second quarter to be split between you and Father," I said. "Then, the third quarter to be split between me and Abby." I looked at Father to see his reaction. Agreeing to share was uncomfortable for him, but he knew there would be a mutiny if he didn't.

"And the last share?" Father asked.

"The rest can fund a share for Louis and be a reserve for one or two additional workers if we need them later, but for now that reserve gets split evenly between the four of us," I explained. Father hadn't blown his top, and we had a solution that made everyone happy.

"Then we divvy up the cash after each delivery?" Amos asked.

"After each one," Father agreed.

"One more thing," I said.

"What's that?" Father asked.

"Abby and I take a week off starting tomorrow morning," I said.

"You just had a week off!" Father exploded. "We have deliveries to make! Why now?"

"I need to see my Grandmother Molly," Abby said. "She doesn't know about my dad yet." Caleb just looked at her and sighed.

"Okay, okay, take your week. How are you going to protect the cash you'll be earning?"

"Remember the new fireproof safe we delivered to the Depot last week?" I reminded him. The clerk's office had burned, and the books burned with it. The Company chewed out the clerk for not having a fireproof safe and sent one to the Depot on the next supply delivery. Luckily, the day's cutting slips were kept in the camp's kitchen. At the end of each day, crew bosses stuffed the slips into a cookie jar. When the clerk finished recording them, the slips went to the storage room off the kitchen, since there was so little room in the clerk's office. It took over a week, but with help from another Company accountant, the ledgers were re-created from those saved cutting slips.

"That was a heavy load," Uncle Amos said. The safe nearly ended up in the lake as it was rolled up the gangplank, on the dolly.

"We shouldn't keep a safe in the house," Father said. "It's the first place the revenooers will search."

"After the barn," Amos added.

"Yes, they'll wreck the barn first. They'll chop up the stills, smash the inventory, and then hunt for the money," Father said.

"There are a lot of places you could keep a safe, places people would never look in," Abby said. We turned to her.

"What did you have in mind?" Uncle Amos asked her.

"We use the old ice-house. We make a hollow by moving some blocks. The hollow will sit behind a row easily moved aside to get to the safe. No revenooer will go to the trouble of moving sixty-pound blocks of slippery ice just to see another wall of blocks behind them." Abby seemed to be studying Father for his reaction.

"That's a good idea," Amos said. Father nodded in agreement. "I need to order one."

"Order two safes," I said. "One for you and Uncle Amos, and one for me and Abby." Father nodded in agreement.

"And one more thing," I said.

"What's that?" Father sighed. He was more than annoyed.

"It's not the 'Nighthawk Distillery.' It can't be that name." I stated. "I don't care what else it's called, but it's not that."

"Fine with me. It was Louis' idea anyway," Father said. "We're not making any money sitting here," Father said. "Let's get those new stills set up this afternoon before you leave. When you two get back from your vacation," he added with attitude, "we'll tackle the ice-house remodel. The safes can be here in a few weeks."

The Ride to Nicatou
Chapter 10

Amos brought us down to the Dam in *The Twilight* the next morning. Bear Dog barked at the loons we saw swimming and diving for fish on the way. We picked up a ride with the cook's rickety wagon from the Boom House to a put-in below Big Pockwockamus Falls. We followed a new road that connected Ripogenus Dam all the way to Millinocket, saving us many miles of paddling. It was rough in places, but the horse drawn wagon sailed through with its big wheels rolling over the wash-outs. We arrived at the put-in just above Debsconeag Falls. As we unloaded the canoe and our gear, the wagon and driver continued to the next lunch site to feed a hungry crew. We hoped we'd be able to catch a ride back up river on our way back, otherwise it was going to be a long trek over land.

The day was beautiful. Diamonds danced on the water, and a light breeze kept the deer flies at bay. Abby and I packed the canoe, tied in an extra paddle, secured our packs, loaded an excited Bear and left the sheltered beach where we had made our lunch. There were several crews working along the river banks as they readied rows of pulpwood to roll into the current on their way to the paper mill. Some were walking on the boom logs along the shore, waving to us as we paddled by. We had paddled a while, listening to a white-throated sparrow whistling from the pointed tops of fir along the shore.

At the mouth of a small stream, we saw boom logs holding back pulpwood. There wasn't a lot of it, and looking up the little tributary I could see open water. That meant there was room for more pulpwood to crowd into the stream before the drivers removed the retaining boom logs and set the pulpwood on their journey over the falls and down the river to the mill in a day or two. We'd be off the river by then. What I couldn't see was that the boom log holding everything back was about to lose its chain and let the pulp wood flood into the main river.

I set an anchor, a rope tied around a rock I found, just above our take-out so we could fish the salmon pool that was above the rapids we would have to carry around. Over the next few hours, we caught and released a few small salmon. At first, they were biting pretty good, but after a half hour passed with no nibbles, we gave up and reeled in our lines.

"Where'd that pulpwood come from?" Abby screamed. The boom must have broken. As soon as I pulled up the stern anchor, a mess of pulpwood came careening around the blind corner above and headed right for us. We grabbed our paddles. Bear barked his encouragement.

"We'll make it!" I shouted at her in the bow. If we were broadsided by fast moving four-foot pulpwood, we'd be sure to tip over. We were a target just like the mechanical rabbit in the shooting gallery at the county fair. We paddled to shore as hard and as fast as we could.

We didn't make it. Our canoe was hammered by the wood, and soon we were swimming above the falls. I saw Bear disappear under a big wave, but he swam to the surface and headed to shore. The canoe with our gear disappeared over the rocks. After we went over the edge of the falls, Bear and I made it to the pebbly beach below. He had no problem getting to shore and started to bark as soon as he shook himself off on the little beach. It was a relief to know that he was on shore and probably okay. I was able to get my footing, but Abby wasn't so lucky. She was thrown to the center of the falls.

"Charlie, I'm going over!" I heard her cry, sculling on her back to keep her feet downstream while checking on the progress of the pulpwood arsenal that had been unleashed behind her. Pulpwood was bouncing off the rocks around her as she arched her back and slid over those granite river-rocks that were water-worn smooth, out of sight. I scrambled down the shore line and grabbed one of our paddles that had washed up on the rocks. They make great splints, I thought, and prayed it wasn't needed for that purpose. I climbed a boulder to look for Abby, my heart about to jump out of my chest. It was difficult enough to have seen Jim Ross floating face down between the logs. There she was, sitting on a pile of logs in the middle of the rapid. A small jam had started to wing out into the current. Bear was barking at her. I calmed him down, and calmed down myself knowing we were not hurt. The south wind had only started to rise but stopped as soon as I got it together.

"You okay, Abby?" I shouted, my hands cupped around my mouth. She stood up and waved. I could see her nodding her head. "I'll look for a rope," I shouted again, and she nodded. The canoe had miraculously shot the rapids without any help and was bobbing peacefully in an eddy along the river's edge just below me. Our packs were still lashed to the thwarts, wet but intact. The canoe wasn't going anywhere for the time being. There was a tar papered storage shed not far off the trail where the Company kept some driving supplies as well as some beans and potatoes. The drivers would be coming along to push any beached pulpwood back into the current, but that might not be until tomorrow. Abby had to get off that small jam now. It was going to be another cold night in the shadow of Katahdin. The temperature had dropped to 38 degrees that same morning and was probably no more than 50 now.

I approached the storage shed. With a lean-to roof, the tar papered structure was built just well enough to last through a mild winter's snow load. The spruce poles that supported the roof had not been peeled. A sheet of canvas acted as a door. Bear stayed on the shore as if to keep watch on Abby. I moved a few small logs that kept the bottom flap from blowing around and tied the canvas back. Strips of bark hung down into the darkness. Spider webs were everywhere. The smell of creosote, tar and turpentine, repair supplies for the bateau, were almost overpowering. I found a coil of rope partially hidden under some canvas.

"That's a relief," I said to myself as I reached for my prize. I found a pick-pole leaning in the corner and grabbed that, too. When I returned to my perch beside the river, I raised an end of rope in one hand and lifted the pick-pole in the other so Abby could see. She nodded. I hurried down the shore. I needed to be just a little closer and stood on a smooth ledge beside the eddy. I could see Abby, and shouted to get her attention. She turned to me and waved.

"I hope she's thinking what I am," I mused out loud. "There's no other way to get her off, right?" I said to Bear. His response was to continue pacing back and forth on the pebbly shore while keeping his eyes on Abby. An occasional growl morphed into a single bark, then a whine, then some nervous lapping up water at the river's edge.

I uncoiled some of the rope. It fed out neatly. Using some thinner rope I had found in a bucket just inside the door, I tied one end near the sharp point of the pick-pole. Next, I let out enough slack so my rescue spear would fly without restraint. I tied the other end of the rope around the tree in front of me. Stepping as far back on the ledge as I could, I hefted the pole, got a balance point, and hurled it with all my strength out and upward toward the jam. The rope snagged on the rock in front of my feet, and my spear fell into the current. I pulled the pole back and reset the rope. I backed up once more. On the second try the pick-pole made it all the way to the jam and embedded its point into the side of a pine log, carrying the heavy rope with it. Bear barked as if he wanted to chase after it.

Abby scampered down the slippery pile of pulpwood and untied the rope from the pole. I watched as she climbed to the top of the pile. When she got to the highest point of the ledge, she anchored the rope around some rusty iron pins from an old dam that had long washed away. I had to give her some slack. The rope sagged, almost touching the water and some straggling pulpwood rushing under it. She was doing exactly what I hoped. The other day we had talked about the cable trolley that was just above the falls. People sitting on the little platform would pull themselves across the river on a cable, high above the swirling waters. Abby was going to do the same thing.

The rope wasn't nearly tight enough. It couldn't be allowed to sag, so I tied it off to a tree beside me. I was able to increase the tension so the rope was taught. Everything held together. The down slope from Abby to where I was standing was really steep. The rest was up to Abby.

Abby took off her belt and looped it over the rope as she climbed down a few logs. The rope and belt were now above her head. With her hands clasped tight to the belt, she pushed off the log. The belt slid her all the way to the shore, her knees bent as she sailed over the rapids. She let go of the belt as she came over the ledge and dropped into the eddy. Bear was so excited at her arrival that he started to swim out her, but as soon as he hit the current, he followed her back onto the shore.

"Nicely done," I cheered. Bear started to wash her face with his tongue.

"Thanks," she smiled. "But please don't ask me to do that again! My belt, can you reach it?" Without her weight pulling it along the rope, it had stopped where she had let go. I found a long stick and hooked it toward us. Abby stood, giving Bear a good scratch around his ears.

"We shouldn't leave the rope like that," I said. "Let's let it go into the river and it might not hang up a boat if one sneaks down this side of the falls." I untied the rope's tensioner while Abby untied the anchors. The rope swung away from shore into the main current, one end still tied to the log jam.

"Charlie, look!" Abby said. She pointed to the rapids she had just glided over. The mist from the water falling over sharp rocks was making a rainbow.

"Aren't rainbows good luck or something?" I asked. Then a double rainbow appeared.

"Looks like twice as much luck coming our way," Abby laughed. Then she stopped.

"What is it?"

"Charlie! Look over there!" She pointed just above the mist. Standing on top of the logs was Moosis. He had the same face paint and spear. But this time the spear tip wasn't clear and shining in the sun.

"Is that blood?" I asked.

"I can't tell," Abby said. "He's in trouble, Charlie. I can feel it." Bear started barking, wading in the edge of the current, his nose pointing toward the log pile as if he could see the figure in the misty bands of color over the rapids.

Moosis beckoned us on. The expression on his face was one of determination. Then he threw his spear at an unseen foe and faded into the rainbows.

"He needs us," Abby said.

"You could be right," I agreed. "We'll have to find out."

We wrung the water out of our soaked clothes before changing into dry ones we had wrapped in oil skin and safely stored in our packs. If we hadn't tied them to the thwarts, the packs would be well down river by now. Abby and I paddled down river to our take-out.

"At least we're close to Molly's village now," I said. We beached the canoe. I grabbed the bow and we rested it upside down on the smooth rocks on shore. We started up the trail to the village green. I began thinking about what was ahead of us, a few more miles to Grandmother Molly's and hundreds of centuries back to Grey Wolf's village.

Bear Dog was leading us as if he knew the way. Shadows flew across the trail ahead, and we heard the *whomp, whomp, whomp* of giant wings cruising overhead. I was thankful for the low leaf canopy that helped hide us from the sky.

"It's following us," Abby said.

"I think we'll be alright as long as we can stay under this canopy."

"But there's the open space all around the fire pit," Abby pointed out.

"That could be a problem," I replied, hoping the Nighthawk

would be gone by then. When we got to the clearing, the wing noises had disappeared. A pig was roasting on a spit in the center fire pit. Two men were slowly turning the spit. When they saw us, they both waved and smiled. It was good to be back. There were several long tables placed around the fire. Hiram was standing with Grandmother Molly by the fire. As soon as Abby saw her, she ran to give her grandmother a big hug.

"Hiram told me about your dad," Grandmother Molly said. "I'm so sorry to hear about him. Are you doing alright?"

"Most of the time," Abby answered. "Having Bear with us gives me a lot of comfort, and Charlie has been a great listener."

"Your father was doing what he loved," Grandmother Molly said. "We all should be that fortunate." They wiped away their tears, hugged again, and turned to the crowd that was beginning to gather.

Members of the clan came out to greet us. Preparations for the evening's feast were nearly finished. Once in a while I looked at the sky overhead, wondering when the razor-sharp talons would come for me, but there was no threat. Bear rubbed against my leg. I felt like I had come home.

"You're safe here with us," Hiram said, sensing my unease. "We have enough power to keep the Nighthawk away." I really hoped so.

Skull Cave

chimney
light shaft over altar
skull face
exit
path to Old Village
enter
cavern
climb
path
light shaft
tunnel
cavern
to present
altar
to past & village
entrance
exit
tunnel
tunnel

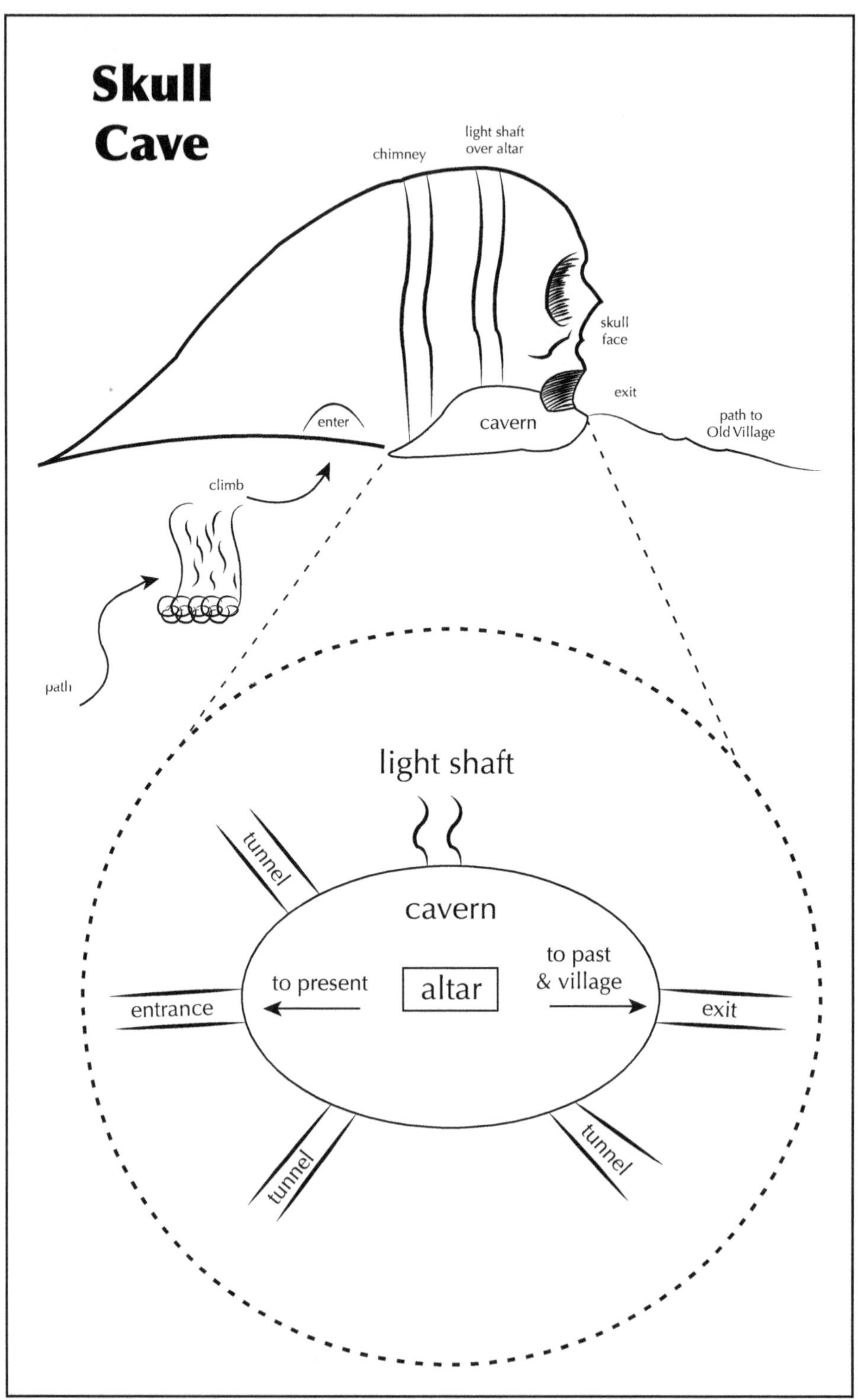

The Pathfinder
Chapter 11

More people began to arrive by various forest trails. Hiram, Abby, Grandmother Molly and I walked the rest of the path to her cabin. Bear led us as if he knew where we were going.

"Hiram told me about seeing Moosis," Grandmother Molly said as soon as we sat at her kitchen table. "What about the black wings? Are they closer now?"

"We could hear them above the canopy on the trail here," I said. "But they disappeared as soon as we came into the village clearing."

"You are the prey, Charlie Bear Claw," Grandmother Molly said.

"I know, but how do I stop it?"

"Clipping its wings will not be enough," Hiram said. "The Nighthawk has to be sealed up in its aerie."

"And how can that happen?" I asked. Wing clipping a Nighthawk wasn't my idea of fun.

"That's a plan we'll have to work on," Hiram said.

"Tell me more about the stone," Abby asked.

"Hiram said you buried the spear point Moosis gave to you?" Grandmother Molly asked.

"When he gave it to me," I answered. "I didn't know how important it was."

"We're lucky we found it," Abby said, handing it to her grandmother. Grandmother Molly looked it over and handed it to Hiram sitting beside her. They were sharing a pipe of tobacco. Hiram went inside. We could hear scrubbing in the sink. Soon Hiram returned with a sparkling clean spear point. He sat down again and put on a pair of wire-rimmed glasses.

"I've never seen you wear glasses," Abby said.

"Once in a while I have to," he muttered, holding the spear point up to the low angled light that streamed in from the setting sun. He seemed mesmerized by how the fading light made it glow.

"Look at the thin lines of black and cream," he pointed out and handed the piece to Grandmother Molly. Five inches long and three at the base, the point had two notches in the sides at the widest part for lashing it to a shaft. The edges were very sharp and slightly serrated. Someone had worked hard on this, and I wondered who.

"Do the lines mean anything?" Abby asked.

"Yes, they do." Grandmother Molly pointed to one of the thin, yellow lines that crisscrossed the piece. These stood out clearly against the dark chocolate color of the stone known as Munsungan Chert or Red Jasper.

"The lines represent the pathways that you are able to see and travel," Hiram said.

"It's like a map?" I asked.

"A map that can get you lost forever," Grandmother Molly replied.

"Like Little Turtle almost did," Hiram replied.

"What happened to him?" Abby wanted to know. Hiram continued.

"Little Turtle was hunting frogs at the edge of the Giant Morass. A path bathed in golden light appeared before him. He had never seen such a pretty trail through the woods, and decided to follow it. The trail now before him quickly disappeared. When he turned to go back, the path there had also vanished. There was nothing but trees and brush. He didn't know which direction he should go. Little Turtle was lost. Days later and weak from hunger, Little Turtle made a bed of marsh grass and slept. When he woke up, he found himself in clean, dry clothes. He was resting on a bed of fir boughs. A cup of warm tea was on a little stand beside him, and he felt eyes watching over him.

"His rescuer tended to his wounds, some nasty scrapes from thrashing through the swamp. She was a sagamore, sachem and medicine woman, a jewel of her clan. It seemed as if there was no injury she could not heal or sickness she could not cure. Boils? Use this plantain. Fever? Make a tea with this willow bark.

"When Little Turtle told the sachem where he was from, she didn't believe him at first because it was so far away. He could not have traveled to her lodge without having taken one of the ancient spirit pathways, and since he was not a true Pathfinder, his journey to her clearing was accidental. She was certain that Pomola was playing games with them. She brought out a small deerskin pouch. Inside was a beautifully shaped spear point. The dark red stone was crisscrossed by narrow, creamy yellow and jet-black lines. Some lines were thick, and others were thin. Little Turtle had followed one of these paths by chance. This was very unusual. The sachem pointed to the stone in her hand.

"'You got here by following one of these pathways,' she pointed to the stone as she moved her finger along one of the black lines slicing across the side. 'The stone should be held in a certain way before a path will appear. But you arrived with nothing to guide you. Who are you?' she asked.

"She got nothing more than a shrug and a shaking head before Little Turtle, exhausted from several nights in the woods alone, fell asleep. The sachem pulled the bear skin over Little Turtle's shoulders and stretched out on her day bed to relax in a band of morning sunlight that streaked over it. She had been up all night nursing his wounds. Soon, the cabin's roof vibrated with their snores. It wasn't long before Little Turtle woke up and looked around. The sachem was sound asleep.

The stone was still on the table inside its little deerskin pouch, the top flap open. Little Turtle swung his legs off the bed, trying not to make any sound to wake his nurse. He took his time standing up, then tiptoed to the table. He eyed the pouch, and with some hesitation, he picked it up and removed the stone. Little Turtle turned it over and over in his hands. Lines that ran across one side of the face met other lines on the other side. Sometimes the lines turned black, and sometimes the lines turned a creamy yellow. He couldn't tell if there was a 'right' side or not. He remembered her telling him that there was a convergence of trails just outside her lodge in the clearing. He wondered if the trails' closeness suggested where she should build her birch bark lodge. Little Turtle placed the stone back in its protective pouch and returned it to the table. He walked outside onto a small, covered porch. But as he stared at the tree line on the other side of the clearing, a well-worn path appeared. It was bathed in golden sunlight as it disappeared into the woods. Little Turtle, curious about where this path would lead him, thought about walking in that direction. 'Maybe,' he thought, 'This will lead me back home to my nest on the river bank.'"

"But he wasn't a true Pathfinder, was he?" I asked.

"No. He could not use the stone, but he had developed the ability to see some otherwise hidden paths. Sometimes this happens. He was about to step onto a path that would take him far into the future when the Sachem, waking up from her nap and discovering her patient was missing, hollered at him to come back or Pomola would catch him. No one wanted anything to do with Pomola, a sometimes cruel but always unpredictable spirit who lived on Katahdin. Pomola would bury Little Turtle in snow even in the middle of summer for the slightest reason. Little Turtle returned to the lodge and was told how foolish he had been."

"How did the stone end up in Grey Wolf's village?" Abby asked. "It's the same one, right?"

"There's only one stone," Hiram explained. "Only a Pathfinder can use it." He handed it to Abby. "This has been part of Grey Wolf's tribe since the beginning of time."

"Sometimes we don't get all the answers we seek," Grandmother Molly said. "The important thing to know is that it's pretty easy to get lost when using this. It belongs with Grey Wolf's people and should be used only in that village's time."

Abby turned the stone over and over, feeling the smoothness of each side. "The lines are all different," she said.

"The thicker lines are well traveled and not as risky. But the thinner lines are not often used and can lead the Pathfinder into dangerous places and times," Hiram explained.

"So why would a Pathfinder want to follow a thinner line?" Abby asked.

"Because sometimes there are no other options. It could be an emergency. Maybe some enemy is after the Pathfinder, and a risky path is the only choice."

"What about the different colors?" I asked. "Some are creamy-yellow and others are black."

"The creamy-yellow lines move the Pathfinder forward in time. The black lines move the Pathfinder back in time. Easy to remember, black is back," Grandmother Molly added. "The Pathfinder holds the stone map up to the Day-Traveler or the Night-Walker. If there are any paths nearby, the stone map will vibrate and the paths will appear."

"How do you two know all this?" I asked.

"I knew a Pathfinder from the old village," Grandmother Molly explained. "She told me all about the stone map."

"Would she still be in Grey Wolf's village?" Abby wondered

aloud.

"She disappeared one day. It was long before the troubles with the Nighthawk, so we all felt she had followed a path and was unable to return to us."

"But how did Moosis get the stone if she and the map were lost together?" I asked.

"My father, Grey Wolf, sent out trackers to find her," said Grandmother Molly. The trackers followed her trail and found the stone map beside a spring where she likely stopped for a drink. She must have seen something she had to get away from fast. She must have gotten on one of the riskier pathways and dropped the stone as she entered it. She would remain in the time when she dropped it, having no means to return."

"Afterwards, the stone was kept safe by the tribe?" Abby asked.

"Until another Pathfinder appeared," Grandmother Molly said. "We didn't know when that would happen."

"I thought that one came along every few generations or something like that," I said.

"That's usually the case," Grandmother Molly said. "But no one came forward."

"So how did Moosis get the stone map?" I asked.

"Grey Wolf must have felt its security was threatened. I think he had Moosis give the map to you for safe-keeping. Grey Wolf didn't seem to be concerned about losing it. Just as Grey Wolf sent me here to be safe, Moosis sent the map far away with you." Abby looked at me. "And you buried it?"

I was pretty embarrassed and didn't know what to say. "I'm sorry, I-I didn't know," was all I could manage. Then I saw Grandmother Molly and Hiram both smile at me.

"It's okay, Charlie. I might have done the same thing, not knowing," Hiram chuckled. I hoped my artifact burial antics could now be a thing of the past. Abby, all business, turned to Hiram.

"If the stone is held up to the sky, it vibrates, I see all pathways nearby, pick one and go?" Abby asked.

"It's that simple, but it only works if a true Pathfinder holds it," Grandmother Molly said. "There is another matter of elapsed time. Maybe you noticed after your last trips back to Grey Wolf's village that more time had passed than you thought?"

"I thought we were gone for days, but Louis said it was weeks. They were going to send out a search team if we had been any later," I said.

"Time passes differently in the present while you travel back in time," Hiram explained. "We don't know exactly why that is, but the hourglass seems to empty faster in the present."

"That's right," Grandmother Molly said. "You could be on a path for five minutes while normal time would be days or weeks. On the riskier paths, it could be years."

"I guess I won't be taking any of those," Abby said. "What about Charlie? He can't see the paths like I do."

"Charlie must follow you closely on any spirit path. If he gets too far away, he would find himself lost in time," said Grandmother Molly.

"If that happened, could Abby find me again?" I asked.

"She would have to retrace her steps, but she should be able to locate you along the path as long as you didn't stray from it," Hiram said.

"Can a Pathfinder choose how far in the past or future to travel to?" Abby asked.

"No, every path has its own time and length," Grandmother Molly explained.

"The stone can be kept safe in this pouch," Hiram said as he reached into his pocket, took out a small pouch and handed it to Abby. Abby secured the leather pocket on her hip and placed the stone map inside. Then she tied down the flap.

"Doesn't the map belong in Moosis' time?" Abby asked. "I thought it might be passed on from one Pathfinder to another."

"The map does belong with Grey Wolf's village," Hiram explained. "As a Pathfinder, you will be able to use it only when you're there, but it must remain with the tribe until they have a Pathfinder of their own."

"But I can still see the spirit pathways?" Abby asked.

"Yes, that will never change. The stone map shows you the nature of the trails, something you wouldn't know without it.

"I know one reason why Moosis has been showing up," Abby said. "He wants us to bring the stone map back to the village. Something must have happened."

"But Moosis isn't a Pathfinder?" I asked.

"No, he isn't," Grandmother Molly replied. "It sounds like there's a need for the map in Grey Wolf's village, but Moosis knows there's only one Pathfinder who can use it. That seems to be you, Abby."

"Remember the map's purpose," Hiram warned. "It is to guide the clan to the best future that it could have. The Pathfinder's job is to advise the tribe about what decisions will create the best future for all."

"If the map has to be returned," Abby observed, "that means we have to make a trip back. Do we have to go right away?"

"You need to go back soon," Grandmother Molly said to Abby. "We don't know if the village is safe from the Stone People. Come, let's get caught up. I want to hear all about our new Pathfinder." She beamed with pride. "Hiram has told me about it, but I want to hear how you discovered this power." Grandmother Molly took Abby's hand, and they strolled off down a nearby trail talking about unintended consequences. Hiram turned to me.

"Tonight, we celebrate Abby Eagle Feather as our Pathfinder. Then, we'll plan what has to be done." Hiram seemed lost in thought for a moment. "Let's you and I get some fish. The perch should be biting about now."

We found some poles, dug a few worms and headed to the perch hole. When we returned, we had a basket of fish to fillet. Grandmother Molly and Abby were arranging the dishes that our extended family brought to the celebration. There were different kinds of salad, the first lettuce crop of the season making its sacrifice. Wild onions, cheeses and a variety of root crops seemed to be common themes.

"We need to get Abby ready for the ceremony," Hiram said. I left. Bear and I went over to the spit to help lug the beast from the roasting pit to the carving table. Bear kept busy licking at the drops of fat that fell from the table. While we were carving, I thought of what this area was like in Moosis' time. We would be using stone knives made from Kineo Rhyolite or from the sharper red jasper, quarried from Norway Bluff on Munsungan Lake. I prefer German steel.

Abby reappeared in costume, beaded moccasins on her feet, a fringe of feathers around each ankle. She wore tasseled deer skin leggings and a fringed deer skin jacket with an occasional colored bead here and there. Her head-dress was a black, shiny stove pipe hat, slightly bent to one side in the middle, as if someone had started to sit on it but had a change of mind just in time. I could see three eagle feathers sprouting from the back. Around the middle of her hat was a gold ribbon, its ends hanging only to the broad brim that almost made it all the way around. Gold rings dangled from her ears. Her eyebrows were wider and her cheeks colored with red ochre. From her neck hung the amulet from Grandmother Molly.

Hiram was also in full ceremonial dress. He wore a vest knitted with beads and small bones. I could pick out a few hawk talons and a long, sharp fang that could only have come from a saber toothed tiger, a fang passed down through the generations, I hoped.

Hiram held a large, shallow bowl. Grandmother Molly placed a braid of sweet grass in the bowl and lit it. When the smoke began to rise, Hiram turned and, with a large eagle feather, wafted the grey plumes of burning sweet grass to the spirits and each of the winds.

Hiram pushed the thick, white smoke to each direction. Hiram took Abby's hand and led her through the smoky air. "May the spirit of Katahdin protect you," Hiram said. Those villagers who accepted Hiram's invitation to join him repeated the phrase. Then, everyone circulated through the sweet cedar smoke as the ceremony came to an end and the eating began.

We had a great feast. Someone's root cellar had been raided, and we had fire roasted potatoes, yams, parsnips, carrots with freshly gathered wild onions roasted together in giant pans.

Later, Hiram, Abby and I were sitting on Grandmother Molly's front porch. There were several rocking chairs. No skeeters or other biting flies could sneak in through the carefully fitted screens. We were stuffed from our feast, but now we had to focus on what was ahead.

"You should get some rest," Grandmother Molly said. "You start your journey to the cavern tomorrow." The cavern at Split Rock was our doorway to the ancient village.

"Just be careful with following the spirit pathways. You don't want to meet up with Pomola," Hiram warned.

We said good night.

"I'm worried, Charlie," Abby said on our way to the bunkhouse.

"You're never worried," I said. "This sounds serious."

"It is. I mean, so much bad stuff could happen. We could get separated in time and never find each other again. I don't think I ever want to go down one of those paths."

"You don't have to go alone," I said. "I'd stay right behind you." I stopped walking and put my hand on her shoulder. "I won't let that happen. If it makes you feel better, we'll tie ourselves together with a rope around our waists, okay?"

Abby turned to me, our arms now tightly around each other. Never would I get too far behind her.

Ndakina
Chapter 12

The Day-Traveler began its journey over Katahdin. I usually woke up with the daylight, and this morning my eyes opened just after five. I looked over at Abby's bunk, but it was empty. I got dressed and went outside to the front porch. Abby was standing in the middle of the clearing, staring at the treed border of the clearing in the rising sun. Mist was lifting from the dewy grass as sunlight crept over it.

"Hey," I shouted to her. "You see any paths?"

"I do," she replied. "There's one right over there," and she pointed to the dense forest.

"Where does it go?" I asked.

"Charlie, I can see the path. It's free of brush and looks easy to walk on."

"But you're not following it, right?"

"No. It's too risky," Abby said. She seemed disappointed and then looked back at me. "Hey, we need to get packed up."

"We're almost ready. We should be able to get going right after breakfast." Abby and I finished loading up and slung the ash pack baskets over our shoulders for the short walk to Grandmother Molly's cabin for breakfast with her and Hiram. Bear Dog knew something was up and didn't stray from our heels.

I could smell the fresh biscuits from the edge of the clearing by her cabin, and my stomach was growling at the thought of Grandmother Molly's baking. We stepped up to her porch and Hiram met us at the door. It wasn't long before blueberry jam was on a buttered biscuit and headed to my mouth.

"I looked for trails this morning," Abby said.

"Did you see anything?" Grandmother Molly asked.

"I did," Abby replied. "Could you please pass the butter?"

"And?" Grandmother Molly prompted as Hiram slid the butter dish Abby's way.

"I just wanted to see what showed up. There's a big difference between what I see and what's there."

"What do you mean?" asked Hiram. He fed a little piece of bacon to Bear. "Ow!" he exclaimed, as Bear snatched it from between his fingers a little too eagerly.

"I see a pathway through the woods. But for anyone else, there's just dense trees and brush. Only a moose could get through it." Abby stopped lathering butter on her biscuit. "How could we even walk through something like that?" she asked. "Please pass the jam."

"When you travel a pathway, there are no brush or uprooted trees to climb around," Grandmother Molly explained. She passed the jam Abby's way. "The experience will be the same for everyone with you."

"How will we know when we get to the end?" I asked.

"You'll know. The paths always end in a clearing," Hiram explained.

"The stone map doesn't work the same way as the amulet," Grandmother Molly said. "The amulet is used in just one place, the altar in the cavern. You've been using it to go to one place at one time. There is no path to follow other than the ones leading to and from the cavern, and those can be seen by anyone. The map reveals other possible routes that can be much more complex, risky and can be seen only by a Pathfinder who holds it."

"There is one more thing," Hiram said. "You might encounter the Stone People on one of your trips back."

"How do you know?" Abby asked. Grandmother Molly and Hiram looked at each other. He nodded his head as if to approve of what she was about to say.

"I hear from the spirits at times. It's more a sense of what is happening then, especially if there's an enemy approaching," Grandmother Molly explained. "The Stone People are migrating from their frozen lands in search of food."

"We'll be watching for them," Abby said.

As Father would say, we were "burning daylight." It was time to be on our way. Bear would be staying with Hiram and Grandmother

Molly. It was too risky to bring him with us. After saying goodbye, we hefted our packs and were off to Split Rock, Skull Cave and the ancient village of Grey Wolf.

....

By that afternoon, we were hopping our way from rock to rock up an old riverbed. We could see a little water trickling between the boulders. Pale and icy blue-green, the water looked like it had been ice not many hours before. Soon, we were at the trailhead that led up to the cavern. The trail cut in back of a fifty-foot waterfall that was three feet wide at the top. It sprayed water everywhere and was pretty loud, probably because it was so far to the clear pool below.

We looked up at the water pouring from the rock. It looked like a broken-off water pipe. We would have to traverse a crevasse that hid behind the falls. The rocks were loose there, and here the spray from the falls made them slippery. Our trek took us behind the falls where the trail led to the cavern and altar inside.

"I wonder what would happen if someone should go over those falls," Abby mused.

"They might survive. The pool below looks pretty deep right where the water hits it."

"I'll have to remember to hold my nose," Abby laughed.

"Of course, you're not doing that, right?" I joked.

"Oh, Charlie, you worry too much! It's the last thing I'd ever do. The only time I get into the water is to cool off when it's hot out." Abby was still chuckling as we scampered across the ledge onto a flat pathway that led to the cave.

"Are you saying our recent canoe upset and your swim over to the log jam was because it was a hot day?" I asked as we followed the trail that led to the other side behind the waterfall.

"No, silly. That wasn't planned." Her response didn't make me feel any less anxious.

We followed the trail into the cave and wound our way into the center of the giant dome of rock. The cavern was huge with several other passageways leading away from it like spokes of a wagon wheel. In the center of the room was a large stone altar. From above, a shaft of light bathed us in a golden color. Abby brought out the amulet and placed it in the small recess that had been made for it many centuries earlier. This was going to be my third trip back, and I looked forward to seeing Abby's ancestors and the friends we had made. But I wasn't looking forward to meeting up with the Nighthawk. There were so many things that could go wrong on this trip that I decided that worrying wouldn't be helpful. That feeling probably wouldn't last, but I wanted to try.

"Ready?" Abby asked. I nodded my head. She reached out for my hand. We had to be touching or only Abby would be making the trip. She followed the ritual that would lead us back to Grey Wolf's time and village.

Abby spoke the words that would turn the clock back to her great-grandfather's time. As usual, there was no indication that anything had happened when she finished. We had to follow one of those tunnels and walk outside to see where and when we were. Once we ended up in a land of ice and snow. Another time it was in a jungle.

Smoke trailing from the longhouses at the base of Skull Cave told us we were in the right place, but something seemed off with the time.

"This isn't when I thought we'd arrive," I said.

"I can see that," Abby replied. It was May when we entered the cavern. Now it was late fall, probably the last half of October. The leaves had changed color to brilliant hues of red, orange and yellow. "Do you think we should go back to the cave and try again?"

If Abby didn't follow the ritual correctly the first time, we'd have to go back to the stone altar and repeat it. Grandmother Molly told us that it might not be Abby's fault. Once we ended up in a frozen, unrecognizable world of ice and snow. "Possibly the spirits weren't listening well," she had said.

"I don't know. It depends on who's in the village. That will give us a better sense of exactly when we are," I said.

We spent a little time with my spy glass to see who was there before heading down the trail. Abby picked out Moosis. He seemed older.

"Moosis looks as old as he was when his spirit appeared to us, doesn't he?" Abby observed.

"He seems ten years older than he was the last time we were here," I said. "Since he looks the same age as when his spirit appeared to us, I'd say we are where we're supposed to be."

I spotted Grey Wolf. I handed the glass to Abby. "Take a look at him and tell me what you think." Abby focused the spy glass on her great-grandfather.

"There are a lot more wrinkles in his face than I remember. I'd say we're ten to fifteen years later than when we were here last," she observed and handed the glass back.

There was no sign of Blackfeather, the incarnation of the Nighthawk, or his lodge that had been covered with crow feathers. A garden sprouted in its place. We decided we were in the right time.

We unloaded all the modern things from our packs and stashed them just inside the cave entrance. It was important not to contaminate the past with items from the future. I kept the spy glass and some matches in a waterproof container, but the clothing we changed into and the pack baskets themselves were authentic for the time, thanks to Hiram and Grandmother Molly. We walked out into the sunlight and into a village that existed thirty-five hundred years before the Katahdin Inn was built.

When villagers learned we had returned, they came out of their long lodges around the clearing to greet us as we entered the village center. Out of the crowd walked Grey Wolf, Abby's great-grandfather, Moosis and Nolka, Abby's aunt.

"Welcome back," Grey Wolf said, and raised his hand in greeting. "It has been a long time." He reached out to Abby.

"It does seem like a long time," Abby said, giving her great-grandfather a hug. "It's nice to see you again." It had been only a month in our time since we last saw each other. But we hadn't returned very close to the time when we were last here. Grey Wolf, Moosis and everyone else had aged at least ten years.

"We got your message," I said to Moosis. "We came as soon as we could."

Then everyone descended on us with many hugs and smiles. After we said our hello's, they invited us to a table of food that had taken some time to prepare. Fall turnip and squash, baked acorn flour biscuits, and a roast something on the spit. Many shared the changes in their lives since we were last together. Nolka, aka Running Deer, told us about her children, grown and gone with children of their own. Little Rabbit had moved to the village of her new husband.
"It's a wonderful welcome," Abby said to everyone. "Thank you all." Abby's Abenaki was much better than mine, so she did most of the talking. After she sat down beside me, Moosis came over to join us.

"You must be wondering about the arrowhead that Moskwaso gave you, Charlie," he said. He reached over to grab a roasted potato.

"It's why we're here," I said. "You were asking us to come back with it, weren't you?"

"It took all the power of a nearby shaman to make that appearance happen," Moosis said. Moosis was much older now. The last time we were together, we were the same age. We never knew exactly when we'd arrive at Grey Wolf's. This visit was at least ten years after the last one.

"When we saw you on the Devil's Staircase, the blood on the spear point really scared us," I asked.

"Sometimes Moskwaso gets a little carried away," he smiled, "but it did work. You're here."

"He's the one who lives at Old Bezo's camp?" I asked.

"He's the one who helped find the aerie on your last visit," Moosis explained.

"Awasosqua told us about your village needing a Pathfinder." Abby handed Moosis the pouch with the stone map.

"We do miss our Pathfinder," Moosis said. He took the stone from its pouch and traced his fingers across the lines on its glassy surface. "She would use this map to help the tribe. We thought about starting a small village by the river, but the map led her to a time not long from now that showed all the trees and dirt had been washed away in a great flood. Only boulders remained. We didn't move there." Moosis passed the stone and pouch back to Abby.

"This belongs to you now," Moosis said. "You are the one who is able to follow its trails." He paused a moment, then looked directly at us. "There is a different threat to our tribe now."

"Greater than the Nighthawk?" I asked. The last time we were here, Blackfeather morphed into the Nighthawk and flew away with Little Rabbit in his claws. We were able to rescue her before she became the monster's lunch.

"There's a tribe from the frozen north who wanders down here once in a while to hunt," Moosis replied. "And they're not hunting game."

"Hiram told us about them. The Stone People, right?" Abby asked. Moosis nodded.

"Soon they'll find our village. We hear they've already emptied out three villages just east of us. Most escaped, but a few ended up on their spit. And they know about the stone map," Moosis said.

"But they can't know where it is?" I asked. "So how can they find it?"

"I'm afraid they are able to sense its location. That's one of the senses they have. Now that it's here, we're going to have to make a plan to greet them properly when they arrive, and do it soon. And they will come looking for it now that you have brought it back home."

"But if the map belongs here, how did Moskwaso get it?" Abby asked. It had been a two-day trip up Chesuncook Lake to Moskwaso's village. There, we fought the Nighthawk and thought it had been destroyed.

"When you were last here, Grey Wolf passed it to me to take to Moskwaso for safe keeping," Moosis explained, "but he didn't want his tribe to be a target so he gave it to you to take it far in the future."

"The Stone People will know the map is here?" Abby asked Moosis.

"They seem to have the ability to locate it. We keep hearing travelers talk about them, but they didn't seem to be moving in our direction." Grey Wolf was sitting across from us. "That will change very soon."

"When you were last here, a hunting party reported that the Stone People were searching for the map," Grey Wolf said.

"But could they use it?" I asked.

"They would be able to. They are very different from us," Grey Wolf replied. "Just after you left with the stone, the Stone People devoured two villages before realizing the map was no longer available. I don't know how they knew, but they did." He looked more tired than I had ever seen him. We arrived more than a decade after our last visit, and Grey Wolf had not aged well.

"How is Awasosqua?" he asked.

"She is well," I told him, "And she wants you to know how much she misses you." Grey Wolf looked away. He had sent his eldest daughter to our time to protect her from Blackfeather, the Nighthawk's human form.

"What time of year did the Stone People come?" I asked.

"Before the Frost Moon," Moosis said. "They were getting hungry and needed to feed before they began their hibernation." I looked at Abby. She nodded quietly as if she were thinking what I was. Snow will be coming soon. We'd have to be done our business before then or we would be snowshoeing and ice-climbing back to the cavern to get back home.

"What do we do now?" Abby asked them.

"Tomorrow we will track down and rid ourselves of these monsters," Moosis said. "We will need your help."

"How can we help?" I asked. "We can't shoot an arrow or chuck a spear."

"Abby is a Pathfinder," Moosis said. "She can lead us right to them. There are hunters who will come with us"

Our meal was at an end and the games were starting. There were ring tosses, races and stories for the young ones. One game was knocking off weighted cones of birch bark from a log. The throwing line was moved back after each contestant cleared off the birch cones with the three stones allowed. After the children tried, grownups took their turns. Moosis knocked off two. Nolka got one after the last of her three stones. The throwing line was moved back quite a distance by the time Abby got up to throw.

"Think you can knock one off?" I asked.

"We'll see," she replied and readied to throw her first stone. Words of encouragement came from the crowd as Abby hurled the first stone. One cone flew off the log.

"All right, Abby!" I shouted. She wound up and threw the second stone. The second birch cone went flying apart in the air. There were more shouts of encouragement. She was now tied with Moosis. His next throw went an inch wide. The onlookers quieted down as Abby wound up for her last chance. She pitched the stone and the third cone exploded. We all cheered her success, even Moosis. In this clan, men were not ashamed of being bested by a woman.

"You should pitch for the Red Sox," I shouted above the cheers.

"Who?" Abby asked.

"Never mind," I said. Some came over to congratulate her. There were no prizes, just a sheet of birch bark with charcoal markings on it. For Abby, an eagle feather was drawn below the beaver tail and otter print that represented previous winners.

Folks were saying goodnights before going back to their lodges. The fire in the village center was slowly burning out when Abby and I headed to the hut reserved for visitors.

"Remember being kept prisoner in one of these?" Abby asked. "I didn't think I'd be sleeping in one just like it."

"Should we really go tomorrow?" I asked her.

Abby put her pack down. "Part of me is scared, but most of me wants to go. Stay close to me, okay?"

"Okay," I said. "I sure don't want to lose you in the timestream."

The Hunters
Chapter 13

The next morning, Abby and I joined Grey Wolf in his lodge. He was seated on a low, fur-covered bench in front of an open pit fire directly under the smoke-hole.

"May the spirits smile on you today," he greeted us, gesturing for us to sit on one of the decorated, woven mats in front of him. Nolka appeared at the door, holding the flap with one hand and a thin piece of wood with several acorn patties in the other.

"How's Mahtagwaysoo, "Abby asked her. "Do you ever see her?" Mahtagwaysoo, or Little Rabbit, had been taken by the Nighthawk on our last trip back here.

"Once in a while," she said. "Little Rabbit has her own family and lives in another village. They all came to the summer potlatch last year."

"Is she still as feisty?" I asked. Little Rabbit was short, determined and brave. She had shown no fear facing the Nighthawk or the monster's human form, Blackfeather.

"I don't think she's changed in any way," Nolka said with a smile. "Her brave has his hands full." Abby and I laughed. You didn't want to mess with Little Rabbit. As Nolka left Grey Wolf's lodge, Moosis and three others entered.

Grey Wolf offered us the tray of food Nolka had brought in. There was plenty for all of us.

"These are the braves who will help us defeat the Stone People," he explained, and then introduced them.

Tomakwa, or Beaver, was short and stout with black hair in

braids tied behind his neck with colorful string. He had a quiver of long, feathered and perfectly straight arrows that hung over his shoulder. In his hand were two beads of stone he kept his fingers busy with. Moulsem, or Red Wolf, wore a red band around his forehead, a red wolf tail hanging down his back over a dark brown deerskin top. He was taller than the others and carried a long spear. Last was his brother, Gesonka, or White Goose who also carried a spear. Long feathers and ermine tails hung from his shoulders. His round face matched his round body and always seemed to be smiling.

"These are for you," Moulsem said as he approached. In his hand were two small leather pouches with lanyards made from deer hide. "They will protect you from your enemies." We thanked him and hung them from our necks. I couldn't say I enjoyed the smell of the asofoedita in the pouch. I remember Hiram calling it "the Devil's Dung." It was supposed to the cure for just about anything wrong with you.

"We're glad you're here," Gesonka said with a smile. "You know the Nighthawk's ways." He turned to Abby. "And now we have our own Pathfinder, too. We hope you will be able to make our hunt a short one." Gesonka handed Abby a dream catcher. "Place this in your pack and keep it above your head when you sleep. Nightmares pass through and go outside. Good dreams flow down the feathers into the person sleeping below."

"Thank you. Nightmares can be scary," Abby said as she placed the fragile totem in her pack. "Why is Gesonka smiling?" she said to Moosis.

"He's always the happy hunter, and he always gets the game," Moosis explained.

Grey Wolf gave us his blessings, and we walked out to the courtyard, leaving him alone in his lodge.

"They are the best hunters of our clan," Moosis said. "If anyone can defeat our enemies, they will be the ones to do it." The hunters looked serious standing there, arms across their decorated breastplates, spears leaning against the longhouse entry. But Gesonka's smile crept back. He couldn't seem to have a serious face for long.

"When do we leave?" Abby asked.

"As soon as we pack," Moosis replied. "We'll leave when the sun is highest."

....

It wasn't long before we were almost running single file along a trail into the woods. We traveled over an ancient riverbed, water trickling deep between the smooth rocks. Sometimes we could hear it running and couldn't see it. Once in a while the cold, blue water bubbled to the surface and we'd have to get our feet wet to continue.

The trail petered out and we were out in the open. There were six of us. The tree canopy had not leafed out yet here, and we had no cover. I heard wings hissing through the air and looked up. Ki'kwa'jenu was sailing over the treetops and swooped down toward Abby who was pushing far ahead of our group. When Tomakwa yelled to look out, it was too late. Moulsem threw his spear that sailed in between the Nighthawk's feathers, landing in the mud beside a pond in front of us.

Abby started to turn to see what was up when the Nighthawk grabbed her shoulders as its wings did backstrokes and flew away with her in its claws, her pack basket dropping to the rocks.

"Abby!" I cried out. "Use your knife." We each had brought a small folding knife we kept on our belts in a special pouch. I could see her struggling to reach it. Meanwhile, Ki'kwa'jenu flew a little higher over the pond. Abby was kicking her feet, and the Nighthawk was struggling to hold on to her.

"We can't shoot arrows because we could hit her," Moosis said as the braves were getting their bows and arrows fitted. At that moment Ki'kwa'jenu circled lower, close now to the water's surface and let Abby go. She came to the surface and breast-stroked to the pond's edge. We ran to see if she was alright.

"Abby, are you okay?" I shouted. By the time I reached her, she had pulled herself up on a flat piece of ledge and seemed to collapse. The Nighthawk was sailing off over the mountains.

"Abby?" I shouted as I reached the ledge shelf. So much for going in the water only when she wanted a swim.

"Ohhh, my arm…." She moaned. "I think it hit the water wrong." She reached over to her shoulder with her other hand. Then she placed her hand to her neck.

"It's gone," Abby said. "Oh no, it's gone. Ki'kwa'jenu took it!"

"Took what?" I asked.

"Our way back to the Katahdin View Inn," she said quietly. She turned her head up to me. "If we don't get the amulet back, welcome to our new home."

"What's gone?" asked Moosis.

"The amulet," Abby said. "Without it, we're not going anywhere."

"Couldn't you use the stone?" I asked.

"It would take so many tries, and we could get so lost," Abby said.

"Nighthawks, like crows, treasure shiny objects and often weave them in their nests like decorations," I said.

"Then we will find your amulet in its nest?" Moosis asked.

"That's where it might be," I said, shifting the small pack basket that had begun to dig into my shoulders. I turned to Abby.

"Are you going to be alright?" I asked. "The arm feeling better?"

"It's calmed down a bit. Let me wring out my foot gear and we'll get going."

I started to put my hand on her shoulder. "You're bleeding," I said. Blood was starting to show on her shoulders where talons had punctured her skin.

"I'll get something for that," Gesonka said, and he scurried off into the tree line. In a moment he returned with a handful of cobwebs.

"These will stop the bleeding," he explained. "We should find some plantain to soothe the wounds." With that, he went on another brief search and returned with a few green leaves which he placed over the cobwebs. The bleeding stopped.

"That feels so much better," Abby said. "Thanks." Gesonka nodded.

Tomakwa, Moulsem and Gesonka went ahead, searching for a high place where we could get a better idea of our surroundings.

"I'm surprised that Ki'kwa'jenu didn't take me to the nest and have me for lunch," Abby said. "I wonder why. It's a hawk and I'm dinner, right?"

"We are all going to be dinner," Moosis said, "if the Stone People can't be stopped."

"I agree," I said. "We have to stop them first. But without the amulet, we're stuck here. We have to find it."

"I'm a Pathfinder," Abby said with new-found confidence. "I'll find a trail that will take us home. I still have the map." I wasn't so sure.

"We may have to rely on it," Moosis said.

"I was hoping we wouldn't have to follow one of those golden paths," I replied. It seemed like such a risk.

The three hunters returned with their scouting report. Gesonka spoke first.

"We saw one of them close up, and did he smell!" he exclaimed. "I was hiding behind a boulder trying not to gag when he passed by just a few feet away."

"What did he look like?" Abby asked.

"His teeth were filed into sharp fangs, like a catamount's. He wore a necklace of what looked like human teeth, a hat made from human skin. His painted face was something from a nightmare. His skin was grey with large scales like a fish. Not someone I would want to meet in the forest," Tomakwa said.

"The Stone People are going to catch up with us soon," Moulsem said. "We could see them coming up the creek bed far below us. They're traveling much faster than we are."

"Maybe it's time to rely on our Pathfinder to get away," Moosis suggested. "If we could find the right path, we will be able to escape their stew pot."

It would be the first time Abby used her skill to locate and follow one of the spirit paths. "Maybe we don't have to," Tomakwa said, now tossing the small stones in his hand. "There's a cave nearby. I think we can get rid of them once and for all."

Then he explained his plan.

"No," I said. "Abby can't be the bait." I was quickly out-voted.

Their plan was to have Abby lure the Stone People into the cave. As soon as they got inside, we would seal the opening. Abby would lead them to the only other exit, and it was such a tight squeeze that only Abby could wriggle through.

"They want the map, know where it is, and seem determined to have it," Tomakwa explained. "She's the only one of us who could make it through the narrow passage at the cave's exit. They're too big to follow, and we're all too fat or too tall to be the bait." He looked at Gesonka's belly with a smile, then to Moulsem who was almost as tall as I was.

"I still don't like it. Can't we do something else?" I asked. No one replied.

"How will we seal the cave's opening?" Abby asked. She seemed alright being the bait.

"It's easy," Tomakwa explained. "We used to hunt bear here. On our last trip, we built a big pile of rock above the entrance thinking we could kill our quarry by letting the rocks fall. But Gesonka wasn't able to lure the bear close enough, so we never let the rocks fall. They're still in place. Once inside, we'll cause a landslide to seal it up. The Stone People will never be able to escape and they won't be able to fit through the exit tunnel. They'll all die there."

I still didn't like the idea; it seemed so risky, but Tomakwa seemed so sure it would work that I agreed.

"We don't have much time," Moosis said. "They're not that far behind us. We should leave for the cave now."

Abby put on her semi-dry moccasins, and we began our climb up the ridge. Anyone following us would probably hear the rocks we sent tumbling down to the pile of scree below us. There was no point in trying to be quiet. I followed Moosis and the others to a shelf just above the entrance. There were a few alder bushes to hide behind. Abby's part was to wait until the Stone People saw her and get them to follow her into the cave. When they were inside, we'd send down the pile of loose boulders to seal the entrance. Abby would scurry to the back of the cave and wriggle out through the back door. We waited only a few minutes before we could see a head-feather poking over a ledge just below us. Then a painted face so grotesque, I felt sick just looking at it. The chiseled teeth were pretty scary, too.

Abby was pretending to fuss with her moccasin when she was about halfway between the cannibals and the mouth of the cave. As they closed in behind her, Abby scurried up the hill and dove into the cave's mouth. A few bats flew out as she disappeared into the blackness.

The Stone People were right behind her. There were eight of them in war paint of different colors. Their scent was so strong my eyes began to water. The first two were now crawling into the cave after her. Six of them were hesitating at the entrance seeing how the first two would fare. Then they crawled in as well. When the last one was inside, Tomakwa gave the order.

"Now," said Tomakwa. Stretched out well above the entrance, Gesonka yanked on the end of a vine-rope. A log flew away from below the carefully hidden pile of rocks just above the entrance, and the rocks came crashing down. The cave's mouth was sealed, and six of the cannibals were buried under tons of rock at the opening. We waited until the dust settled to be sure the six were done for. There was no movement. We climbed over to where the narrow exit was. We could hear the two remaining ones inside. The coughing we could hear told us that they were close to the exit tunnel. They were probably trying to get some relief from all the dust, and I thought I could see part of an angry face between the rocks as if looking through the bars of a jail. But this was more than their jail. It would soon become their charnel house.

"Where's Abby?" I asked. "She can't be inside, can she?"

Tomakwa shook his head. "No, they'd have killed her right away, and we didn't hear anything."

I was beside myself. "But where is she? We have to go in there and find her," I said and started to pull a boulder away from the exit. Gesonka grabbed my arm.

"We have them where we want them, and they are never coming out," Gesonka said. "We must leave them there."

"But she's still in there. I can feel it," I said. The south wind was starting to move the tree tops and dust was blasting up the side of the mountain. It takes Abby's calming voice to get me to stop Sowanakik from uprooting trees, but she wasn't here.

A voice came from the trail below us. "Hey, everyone. Are they all trapped in the cave?" It was Abby. She seemed to appear from nowhere, walking up to us on a narrow game trail.

"Abby! How'd you get out? I thought you were inside! Are you okay?" I asked. I ran and hugged her tight.

"You have no idea how worried I was," I told her. She hugged me back.

"I do know," she said. "You've summoned Sowanakik, and you only do that when you're angry or stressed out." The wind was dropping.

"We weren't worried," Moosis smiled. "We hunters know the power of a Pathfinder."

"The Stone People are finished for good," Moulsem said.

"How did you escape?" I asked Abby. By now the others were smiling as if they knew how she escaped. I thought I could hear Gesonka chuckling.

"I found a spirit path at the very end of the tunnel and followed it," Abby explained. "I ended up in a little clearing just over there. Sorry I scared you. I had to climb up here from where the path ended."

"You couldn't have wriggled through the rocks at the exit?" I asked.

"There wasn't time," she said. "Two Stone People were buried in the landslide, but the rest were right behind and could have captured me. When I saw a path in the cave right in front of me, I dove into it, hoping it would lead me back here. Are you okay, Charlie? You look pretty pale."

"I thought we lost you," I said with a sigh of relief and sat on a nearby boulder. "I'm fine now." I looked at Moosis.

"It's time to get the amulet back," I said.

"We need to go back to the village to get the supplies we need," Moosis said. "Then, we'll head up the lake to Moskwaso's village and the aerie." I nodded my head, and soon we were on our way back to

Grey Wolf's village.

Moskwaso
Chapter 14

"We have to find the Nighthawk soon," Abby said as we sat down for a short rest. "The longer it takes, the more likely we'll never find the amulet."

"It will take the rest of the day to get back to Grey Wolf's, another day to get on the water, and half a day more to paddle to Moskwaso's if there's not much wind. Then we have to get to the aerie. That's too long a time," I pointed out.

"And if the wind comes up, it could take longer," Gesonka said. "Once we were stuck on an island for two days with a north wind that made two-foot waves. Just after the wind died down enough to safely paddle, it turned direction and blew the other way just as hard for another three days."

"We were stuck on that tiny island for five days in all," Tomakwa said. His long braids bounced over his shoulders as he spoke.

Abby seemed lost in thought. "What do you think, Abby?" I asked.

"There might be a way to get there faster," she said.

"How?" I asked.

"We could use the stone map," she suggested. Moosis and the hunters nodded their heads. "If we took the right trail, we could even be there before the Nighthawk returns to its nest."

"We don't need to go back to Grey Wolf's," Moosis said. "We can get anything we might need from Moskwaso."

"Shouldn't we let Grey Wolf know the danger from the Stone People has passed?" Abby asked.

"Yes, he should know soon in case they were planning to hide. We don't know how long we'll be hunting the Nighthawk," Moulsem said. He was smoothing out the red wolf's tail that hung from his shoulder.

"If I can find a short path that will lead me back to Grey Wolf's, I could deliver the message and meet you at the put-in," Abby said.

"That will save a lot of time," Moosis said.

"But you could get lost in one of those paths," I pointed out.

"We don't have much of a choice, Charlie," Abby said. "If we don't get there fast, we could lose the amulet forever."

"And if the Nighthawk figured out how to use it, then no one would be safe," Tomakwa said. "She's right."

"I don't like it," I said and stood up.

"I don't either," Abby said. She reached for my hand. "But we have to take that chance. I'll be careful, Charlie." And Abby took the stone from its pouch on her waist. She pointed it to the tree line and turned in almost a full circle. "I see several paths," she reported. "But only one of them will take me there."

"Same time?" I asked.

"Same time," she said. "The path looks like it's pretty short."

"Be careful," I asked and gave her a hug goodbye.

Abby started off for the trees and soon disappeared into the forest. The rest of us began the short trip to the lakeshore where the canoes were kept. If Abby didn't meet us there, we'd have to head up the lake without her once the wind quieted down.

It started raining, and the trail we were following became muddy and slick. With mud-covered leggings, we arrived at the mouth of what I knew as Mud Brook.

"Took you guys long enough," a voice came out of the forest. It was Abby with a big smile on her face. "What, were you taking naps along the way? Tired out or something?"

"Abby!" I shouted, and ran to give her a big hug. "You made it. I was so worried."

"It wasn't hard at all," she reported. "The path I found led me directly to the village. I found Grey Wolf and let him know they were safe from the Stone People and what we were going to do next. He sends his greetings and wishes us success, by the way."

"Was the traveling easy?" Gesonka asked.

"It was really easy walking and it hasn't taken me any time at all to get here," she replied.

We were quiet for a moment. I was thinking about the power of a Pathfinder with a map.

Moosis broke the silence. "The north wind is still pretty strong. We won't be able to paddle into those waves until it dies down."

"How long?" Tomakwa asked as he scratched under his beaver tail breast shield.

"This wind could last for days," Moosis answered as we stared at the angry waters.

Slate grey in the south, dotted with white caps, the lake was as rough as I think it could be. Winds were gusting over thirty-five miles an hour. I could see sharp, cresting waves that were at least three feet to the foamy peaks. But looking south, only the backs of the waves were showing, and things seemed deceptively calmer. Moosis was right. We weren't going anywhere until the front passed.

"I wonder if you could counter that wind with a little Sowanakik," Abby mused.

"I wouldn't want to try it. I'd have to stay focused all the way up the lake to Moskwaso's," I said. "I don't think I could do it, and if I weakened any, we could be in trouble pretty fast.

"I could find a path," Abby offered. We all looked at her.

"With us in tow?" Gesonka spit out. His face showed an unconvinced mind that it would be a great idea.

"Yes, of course. You'd have to stay really close to me or you could get lost in the timestream," she explained.

"See what you can find," Moosis said. "We will tie us together so we won't spread out."

Abby walked to a little clearing beside us. It looked like a forest fire had done its work not long ago. Red fireweed was sprouting high around the charred stalks of what trees remained standing. Blueberry bushes had popped up here and there. She pulled the stone map from its secure pouch and began to turn slowly, holding it at waist level and pointing it at the forest as she turned.

"There are three that lead to Moskwaso's village," she said.

"That's good," Moosis said. I wasn't so sure.

"What are they like?" I asked.

"One goes to the past, and the other two stay in the present," Abby explained.

"Both go to the same place and time?" Moosis asked.

"Just one. I think the other may end up too far in the future," she said.

"Far enough for us to get home?" I wondered aloud.

"Sorry, Charlie, but it's way beyond our time," Abby said, reaching over to me.

"We have one path to take," said Moosis. "We'll get something to keep us together," The hunters went off to see what they could find.

I looked at Abby who was holding my hand. "I really love you, Abby," I said. "I can't imagine losing you, so please, please, keep me close so I don't get lost?" I squeezed her hand.

"I love you, too," she said. "You won't get out of my sight while we travel." She squeezed back.

Moosis and the hunters returned carrying what looked like rope. It was actually coils of pliable vine. We tied the vine-rope around our waists so we were all behind Abby, the same distance apart. I wondered how far away from Abby was too far, and I felt pretty glad to be right behind her.

While we were roping ourselves together, Abby walked through the tall grass toward the forest. I could see her studying the stone map. Soon, we were all strung together. Because we were all roped together, all of us could see the golden sun-lit path that snaked away through the woods.

"Everyone ready?" Abby asked. We nodded our heads. "Keep an eye on the person behind you, and shout out if they suddenly go missing." With that, we were on our way.

It was easy walking, and the trail was pretty, bathed in golden sunlight and lined with trees I had never seen before. Some were giants, and others were in different colors. Some smaller bushes sported giant leaves that seemed poised to reach out to grab our legs but leaned away as we passed. A few critters scampered across the path. The color of their fur, or maybe it was feathers, was varied and bright. I could see claws and teeth. I didn't recognize their tracks or scat. We kept moving, nearly in lock-step since we were tied together.

The recent rains had left the streams and rivers swollen, and the little brook the trail followed was roaring with whitewater. We couldn't hear each other without shouting even though we were tied together a few feet apart.

Moulsem was at the end of our human chain. I could see the red wolf's tail bouncing as we walked whenever I turned around to check. With the roar of the brook, there was little talking as we found our way. We stepped into a clearing that was used as a garden. Pumpkins were along one side. Squash had grown up the now brown stalks of corn, but it had all been gathered. I could see some of the village on the other side, wisps of smoke rising in the stillness of late-fall air.

"Hey, where's Moulsem?" Gesonka asked. We turned to see him dangling the end of the tether that had been around Moulsem's waist.

"Oh no!" Abby exclaimed. "When did you see him last?"

"Just before we entered this clearing," Gesonka replied. "We have to find my brother."

"Not you guys," she said. "You all stay put. I'll head back to look. I just hope he hasn't gone off the trail or we'll never find him."

Abby took out the stone and located our path the woods seemed to have swallowed up. She walked back between the trees. It wasn't long before she returned. Moulsem wasn't with her.

"He must have gone off the path," Abby said. "I found his tracks and an arrow poked into the ground as a marker, but no other sign of him." She brushed off some burdocks clinging to her leggings.

"Will we be able to find him when we come back?" Moosis asked.

"I'll take another look," Abby replied. "But I just don't know. If the arrow is still there when we return, we might be able to find him if he doesn't stray too far off."

"We have to get to the aerie," I pointed out. "We don't have time to find him." The hunters were nodding in agreement.

"He knew the risks," Moosis said. "We need to move on and try later."

We ditched the vine around our waists and walked through the woods to Old Bezo's village. The last time we were here, he introduced us to the village shaman, Moskwaso. The longhouses looked the same except for a couple of new ones. The village was thriving. Our first stop was to call on Old Bezo, the village chief. Several villagers greeted us warmly. Moosis' cousins were nowhere to be found, and there were only a few residents visible. They stopped and stared at us, popping back into their homes as if they were in fear of something. I didn't recognize any of them.

I could see the huts neatly spaced along the edge of the open yard when Abby stopped in her tracks near the fire pit.

"The Nighthawk has been here," Abby said.

"How do you know?" I asked.

"I just sense that as I pass over the spot where something has happened, like when I sensed where *The Tethys* went down," she said. "The Nighthawk grabbed her shoulders from behind. She never saw it coming." Abby paused a moment in thought. "I don't think she made it."

We came to the entrance to Old Bezo's longhouse. Leaves had collected in front of the door. Spiderwebs and the remains of a huge wasp's nest hung above it. No one had gone inside for some time.

"Maybe we should find Moskwaso. He'll know what's going on," Moosis said. His hut was down at the other end of the clearing. As we approached, we could see him cross-legged in front of his doorway grinding away with a stone pestle and bowl.

"You have returned," Moskwaso said in a deep voice that I remembered, smiling at us. Long, black braids of hair flowed from his feathered birch bark hat. His dark eyes scanned our group. "And you have brought hunters? We have been expecting the Stone People. We could use some help." Moosis introduced the rest of our group.

"The Stone People are no longer a threat," Moosis told him. "They have been destroyed." When he described how we had done it, Moskwaso seemed pleased.

"We stopped in to see Old Bezo," Abby said.

"He walks in the spirit world now," he looked down as he answered. "He began that journey during the Planting Moon." He looked up at Abby.

"You have the map," Moskwaso said, gesturing to the pouch on her hip. He turned to me. "I knew I gave it to the right person for safe-keeping."

"You might not think so when you hear what he did with it," Abby said. I think I groaned with embarrassment, wishing Abby would just forget about it.

"Charlie buried it," Moosis explained. "Just so he could find it after he got home." Moskwaso raised his eyebrows and smiled.

"I expected that," Moskwaso said. "I was confident it would not be lost." I felt a little better hearing that. "How did you get here?" He pointed to the lake. "I don't see any canoes on the beach."

"We took a path," Abby explained, patting the pouch that kept the stone map safe. "But we lost one of our hunters on the trail. We don't have time to look for him right now. We have to get to the aerie." Moskwaso had helped us last time we were here, and we were hoping for his help again.

"Maybe you will find him on your way home," Moskwaso said. "Why did you come?"

"The Nighthawk took my amulet," Abby said. "We hope to find

it in the aerie."

"How long ago?" Moskwaso asked, scratching his neck.

"Not long," Abby answered. "I hope that we get there before the Nighthawk brings it back to its nest."

"Where are my cousins?" Moosis asked. "I see their longhouses have not been occupied for a while," as he gestured across the yard.

"There is trouble again," he said. I'm sorry to tell you that Old Bezo wasn't our only loss. It was the Moon of Falling Leaves when it happened." He paused and sighed. "The Nighthawk took one of our young maidens. Your cousins and three of our bravest hunters went to recover her, to slay the beast with wings and to destroy all the eggs. Now they all walk with the spirits and Old Bezo." Moskwaso again lowered his head.

"And the Nighthawk?" Abby said.

"The Nighthawk survived. We saw it fly from the aerie," he said. "Hours passed, and when the braves did not return, we suspected what had happened. Several of us climbed up to the aerie to bring our brothers and sister home. There had been a big battle. Broken arrows and spears littered the giant nest. The only sign of our maiden was a necklace. But the braves did not destroy the hatchlings and the eggs. We think they died before they could. Now, there is only one Nighthawk remaining." He looked directly at Moosis. "You should go now," he said, "Before it returns. Then you might surprise it."

"That's not all we're going to do," Moosis said. "This time, we will destroy it for good." Gesonka and Tomakwa nodded with determination.

"There are some spears and arrows over there," Moskwaso said, pointing to the corner of his home. "Take what you need, and may the spirit of Katahdin keep you safe."

Our hunters gathered the weapons they needed, and I took a stout spear. Then, we were off to the aerie.

We walked through the resting place. A recently built platform with ornate decorations hanging from its four pillars was most likely Old Bezo's resting place. There were five more beyond it, black nighthawk feathers dangling from their beds. The path through the resting place was decorated with rose quartz all along its border.

The hunters stopped and faced the rows of biers. Crossing their right hands over their hearts, they chanted briefly. I couldn't make out the words. It wasn't long before we were looking up at the aerie's opening in the cliff that loomed far above us.

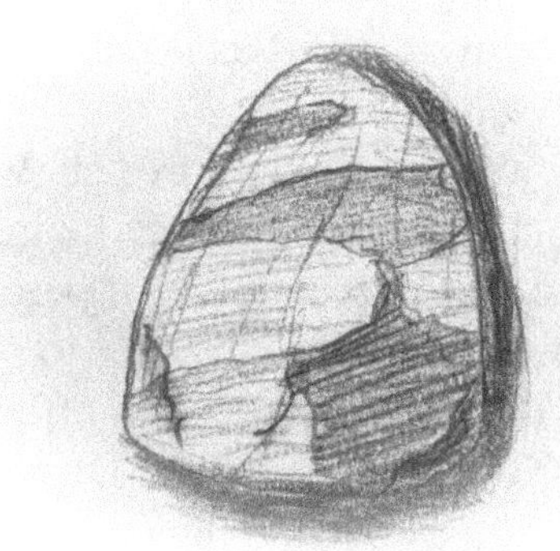

The Nighthawk
Chapter 15

At the hunters' request, I sketched the aerie's floor, where the nest might be, and indicated the size of the main entrance. They made their plan. Then, we studied the trail that led up the side of the cliff.

"The best place to climb is in that crevasse," I said as I pointed to the trail Abby and I had taken on our last trip here. "The rocks are loose at first, so we'll need to be careful not to send one down on top of the head below us." The hunters studied each other for a moment, wondering which one would be the last in the line. The climb didn't take long at all with Moosis leading the way. The hunters seemed different than they were on the trail somehow. They were clearly focused on what had to happen and understood the risks. Grips of iron on the rocks, determined looks on their faces, we climbed the chimney. No one spoke as we silently gathered at the rear entrance to the aerie and peered around a huge boulder to catch a glimpse of the giant nest.

Beyond the nest and at the left side of the main opening in the cliff, a short wall of ledge jutted out several feet towards the center. And on the right side, a pile of broken ledge that had fallen from the aerie's ceiling rose several feet.

Sharp spears in their hands, Tomakwa and Moosis positioned themselves at the left side behind the jutting wall. Gesonka and Abby hid behind the pile of broken ledge at the opposite side. Gesonka had his bow ready, and Abby collected several fist-size rocks in a pile beside her. I stood just beyond the giant nest where there were several intact, giant eggs. I was the bait this time, making my job the easiest. All I had to do was hide below the nest's lip and stand and wave my secret

125

weapon at the beast when it landed in the aerie's opening. I had a spear in case I needed it, my only protection. The wait, short as it really was, seemed to take forever.

It wasn't long before we heard air streaming through wing feathers like the wind whispering in the pines as the Nighthawk circled back and forth. It seemed to be checking out the aerie before it perched in the opening. My job was to raise Sowanakik, my South Wind, to push the beast into the opening of the aerie. It didn't take me much effort to make a southern gale push the Nighthawk into the opening. Dust was everywhere, bat guano peppering us as the gusts blasted the cavern.

And then it landed, dust rising up around it nearly hiding it from view. The wind died down as I focused on what was standing in front of me. I held the gaudy glass-bejeweled cross high above me. What light came in through the entrance revealed the swirling clouds of dust and illuminated the cross. The Nighthawk looked right at me. Shivers went up and down my spine. If our enemy had been a vampire, the cross would have chased it away, but that was not the plan. We wanted it to come all the way to the nest, and my lure was working. Stepping slowly toward the far side of the nest, the demon hissed at me.

"Tell me, Charlie Bear Claw, how does it feel to know you will soon lose your power and your life at the same time?" it rasped. I could see Abby's amulet still grasped in its claws wrapped around two of the three talons on its foot. It cocked its head and stared at the cross I was holding.

"What is this pretty thing?" it hissed, tipping its beak in the direction of the cross.

"It's a present just for you," I teased, tilting it in my hand. As planned, Abby stepped out from her hiding place and pitched a stone that slammed the Nighthawk in the back of its head, stunning it. When it turned to Abby's direction, she hit it again with a loud thwack. The beast turned back to me and staggered closer, blood trickling down the side of its head. Abby stepped back, two more stones in her hands while Moosis, Tomakwa and Gesonka hurled their sharp spears at the beast. The Nighthawk fell in my direction, and I was ready. As soon as Abby stunned it with her first throw, I dropped the cross and readied my spear by planting the shaft in the dirt, holding it up at an angle. The Nighthawk staggered toward me, three spears buried in its black feathers, and fell hard, my spear piercing its chest as the black wings covered me for the last time. I crawled out from under its weight, following the rim of the nest.

As we watched, the beast hissed its last breath, and like the early morning fog in September, slowly evaporated into a white mist.

"We have to break these eggs," Gesonka shouted. One was beginning to crack open.

"I can see a beak," Abby shouted, and nailed the hatching egg with two stones, one right after the other. The stunned hatchling was quickly dispatched by Tomakwa while Gesonka pierced the remaining eggs with his spear.

There was silence. The beast was gone and there were no descendants to take its place.

"Everyone okay?" Abby asked.

"We're alright," Moosis said as he looked at Gesonka and Tomakwa. "It is done." With that, he picked up Abby's amulet, unwinding it from the twigs of the nest where the beast had dropped it. "This is yours," he said, handing it to her.

"Thank you," Abby said, placing the leather loop over her head. The amulet was our ticket home.

"Look," Tomakwa said, pointing to a tail from a red fox. It was beside one of the crushed eggs.

"That's Moulsem's," Gesonka said. He picked it up and handed it to Tomakwa for confirmation.

"But we lost him on the spirit path," Abby said.

"There's no question. See this white spot?" Gesonka pointed out, turning over the tail. "This is his for certain."

"He may not be walking with Pomola now," Tomakwa said. "There's no blood on it. Moulsem could still be stuck on that path."

"And we could still find him," Abby said. "Maybe I can find the same pathway back."

"Let's get out of here," I said. "I can't stand the smell anymore." Tomakwa tucked the red fox tail into his waist band, and we climbed down from the aerie into a bright, sunlit afternoon.

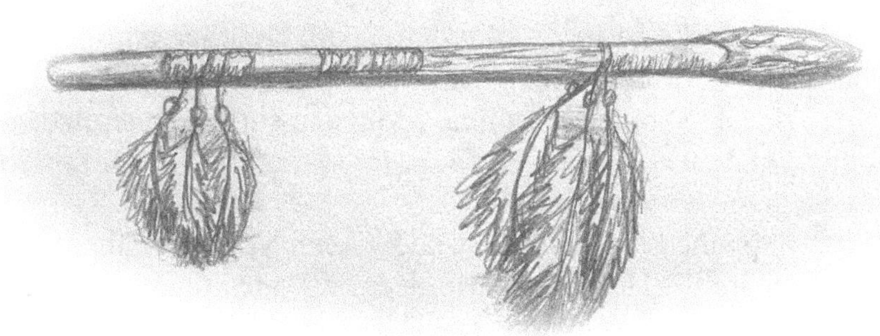

One Way Back
Chapter 16

"You have done well," Moskwaso praised us at the little celebration. Cooking fires were going in most of the longhouses as the villagers had prepared a meal to celebrate our victory.

"You will never be troubled by the Nighthawk again," Moosis said.

"Or the Stone People," Moskwaso pointed out. "Now, let's see what kind of moose hunters you are!" Everyone laughed. We stuffed ourselves and said our goodbye's. After we walked to the edge of their courtyard, Abby consulted her map.

Abby thought she found the same pathway we followed on our way in. I don't know how she could tell. They all looked the same.

We were all tied together, a few feet apart as before. Now it was Gesonka at the end. We were all keeping a sharp lookout for any sign of Moulsem. It wasn't long before we came to the bank of a wide and rocky stream. There was white-water as far as we could see.

"This isn't the same way," I said.

"We must have taken a wrong turn," Abby seemed upset. Then she turned to me. "Promise you'll stay close? I couldn't bear to lose you."

"Don't worry, I'm like glue," I said. "But if this is a wrong turn, will we still find Moulsem?" Gesonka and Tomakwa stood still, hoping to find him.

"I think I saw a fork not far back. Let's head back just a little," she said. "Even though he could have come this way. I just hope he didn't move." We maneuvered around with the rope still connecting us and re-traced our steps.

"There's the fork I missed," Abby said, pointing to the side. "We need to head this way." She turned down the path and there sitting on a rock we could see Moulsem in the golden sunlight.

"There he is!" shouted Gesonka. Moulsem stood and smiled.

"I thought you'd never get back, my brother," he said. "Got anything to eat? I'm starving."

"What happened?" Gesonka asked. "First you were there and then you disappeared!" He passed Moulsem a water flask and some venison jerky.

"The rope slipped off my waist," Moulsem said in between chews, "and you were running too fast to hear me with the roar of the stream we were beside. Then the Nighthawk swooped down on me. I ducked, but it was only able to snatch my fox tail off the back of my head and flew off."

"You mean this fox tail?" Gesonka smiled, holding up Moulsem's totem we found in the aerie. "We thought you were dinner."

"How....." Moulsem started to say, canteen stopped midway to his mouth. Moosis explained what happened as the other two acted it out. After the warhoops subsided, we tied the rope to our discovered hunter for the trip back to Grey Wolf's village. On this trip, Moulsem was not at the end of the line.

The path ended in the courtyard of Grey Wolf's village. When we emerged, everyone rushed out to greet us with smiles and cheers. There was quite a celebration that night. There were many reenactments of the battles we had fought. The hunters set up a row of birch bark cones that Abby picked off, one rock at a time. No one could beat her. In one re-enactment, A Nighthawk statue was made just for this celebration. Abby knocked off its beak with one stone and caused its head to explode with a second.

While we were waiting for the dancing to begin, Nolka came over to visit with us.

"I am so relieved you have returned," she said. "So many of us were afraid you wouldn't make it back."

"We were careful," Abby said. "And a few steps ahead of our enemies."

"How is my sister?" Nolka asked. Since Abby's Grandmother Molly and Nolka were sisters, that made Nolka her great aunt.

"She is well," Abby replied, "but she's getting older. It seems a little harder for her to get around. She stays home to tend the garden and doesn't travel anymore. She seems happy with Hiram. They're good together."

"It is not easy to find a good man," Nolka mused.

"There are some around," Abby replied. "You just have to keep looking." The young women laughed.

"Awasosqua thought she found one," Nolka said.

"When was that?" Abby asked,

"A moon or two before she left. She liked him a lot. Grey Wolf was worried they might run off together." Nolka smiled. "Of course, she would never do such a thing."

"Was he handsome?" asked Abby.

"He was good looking, a large man, very light skin and a long red beard and a leather hat in the shape of a cone with horns on each side. I had never seen one like it before. He carried a long knife that could break stone. I saw him make fire with that knife and a stone he carried in a pouch. I remember when I first saw him. Awasosqua and I were just coming back from a swim when we heard a sound on the trail and decided to hide. He passed by us on the way to the lake. We followed him to see what he could be up to, but we weren't too quiet." Nolka paused. "He turned around just in time to see us peek out from a tree behind him and called us out."

"Did he have a name?" Asked Abby.

"He said his name was Erik. He stayed a little while, maybe a moon. He left on a hunting trip just before Blackfeather moved himself into the tribe. He said he came from a land far away beyond the sea. No one has seen him since," Nolka explained.

As I wondered about that Erik, Olive's nephew Erik, and Abby's red hair, the conversation turned to other things, the harvest celebrations, drying venison and moose meat, and packing enough food for a winter's visit to their sister clan on the coast. Neither Abby nor I really heard much of it in between thoughts of the red-haired man and a young Grandmother Molly meeting in Grey Wolf's village so long ago. I looked at Abby.

"The red hair would explain a lot," I said. Abby was lost in thought. "Abby?" She turned as if hearing me for the first time.

"Let's get settled in for the night," I said, and we walked to the guest lodge.

· ·

"What are you thinking about?" I asked Abby after we settled in at the guest lodge for the night. "You seem lost in thought."

131

"I have to wonder," Abby said. "The timing, the red hair, it all seems to fit too well."

"You might want to talk to Grandmother Molly," I suggested. "She'll tell you what you need to know." We left it at that. But I couldn't seem to quiet my thoughts about our travels along the path. I wondered why it seemed so easy to find Moulsem.

"He stayed put," Abby said. "He didn't wander for water or food."

"As he was told," I said. "So, if I go missing on one of these hikes, you'll be able to find me as easily?"

"As long as you do as you're told, Charlie Bear Claw. Come here, you." Abby reached out for me, her hand pulling my face to hers. I started to say something but was quickly quieted.

The next morning was as beautiful as a late fall morning could be. The spiders had been busy all around the bushes that bordered the village center. A heavy dew had formed on each spider's web, making each one seem like a piece of intricate white lace. Like snowflakes, or the paths that Abby saw, no two were alike. Some ground fog was misting up through the bare branches of the birch and poplar, the first leaves to fall. Soon, the ground would be white and hard, and so would the lives of these villagers, covered with snow and struggling to eat. Most would travel to the coast for the winter, but some would remain to hunt moose. We packed our things and looked for Grey Wolf. We found him sitting outside his longhouse chipping away at a new Munsungan chert spear point.

He looked up as if he heard us before we appeared.

"We're on our way home," Abby said. "Any message for Awasosqua?"

Grey Wolf looked over at the hut across the large yard and pointed. "Nolka told me you talked about Erik. He stayed over there for about a month, then he was gone. They liked each other a lot. This was just before the trouble with Blackfeather when I sent Awasosqua to your time to save her life. Awasosqua had given up any hope of seeing him again, and started a family with one of the men in her new tribe almost as soon as she arrived."

"That's good to know," Abby said. "Tell me, what happens to the stone map now that we're ready to head home?" Abby took the stone from her hip.

"The map goes with the Pathfinder, whoever that is. You may

take the map with you as no one else here has the powers to use it."
Abby nodded and returned the stone to its pouch.

We said goodbye to Grey Wolf and went into the bright sun of the courtyard. Moosis was walking toward us. His white boned breast plate and dark beads that drooped over it glistened in the sun, or maybe it was his smile that brightened the day.

"Moosis," I said, reaching out to grasp his forearm as he grasped mine. This was how one shook hands here. I felt so fortunate to be counted as his friend. "You look like you're off for another battle." Abby ran over to give him a hug.

"Just a moose hunt," he said. "Want to come along?" He looked at both of us. He was serious, too. Abby and I looked at each other, then back at him.

"How could we leave now and miss a moose hunt?" I asked Abby.

"I don't think we can go home now, do you?" She said. So, we went on the hunt with Moosis, Gesonka, Moulsem and Tomakwa for one last adventure together.

. . . .

Two days later, we were up the trail to the cavern. It was still a steep climb, and we had to stop once in a while to get our breath. We could see the village below us, residents sweeping yards, hauling water, and preparing food. Smoke wisped from the longhouses. Children played. It was a quiet moment, each of us in our own thoughts about what we had accomplished.

"Let's get going," I said. "We're burning daylight and I would like to be on the other side of that cave up there." Abby took my offered hand and we continued up the trail.

We reached the cave and walked inside. Abby placed the amulet on the depression in the stone, and while we held hands, she recited the words that brought us back to Grandmother Molly and Hiram.

The Waterfall
Chapter 17

We followed the trail across the ledge and crept carefully over the slippery rocks behind the waterfall. There must have been heavy rain as the roar was unusually loud this time. I was following Abby and was looking for better footing when I heard her scream. I looked up in time to see her sliding fast down the sloping ledge.

"Charlie!" she screamed. She disappeared into the waterfall that cascaded before us. I shouted for her, but she couldn't hear with all the noise of tons of falling water. I scurried over the rest of the path and came out to a sunny, warm summer morning.

"Abby!" I shouted. There was no answer. I looked over the boulders along the trail's edge. I could see the deep pool the waterfall dumped into, and there in the middle, splashing about like a playful otter, Abby was making her way to shore.

I was out of breath by the time I got down to her and kneeled on a flat rock that overhung the pool. "Are you okay?" I asked.

"I'm fine, but my backpack isn't," she said. "Boy, that ledge was greasy." She was jumping on one leg to dislodge the water in her ear. I looked out to the pool of water and could see it bobbing about. "I'm already wet, so I'll go get it," she said. Abby swam out a bit, grabbed a shoulder strap and pulled the backpack to shore.

"Here," she said handing me a strap. I grabbed at it to pull it ashore, but it seemed to pull back. Before I knew it, I was in the water with Abby and the pack basket. When I came up, we had the required splashing and dunking trials and crawled out on the flat rock I had recently vacated. We started hanging wet clothes on alder bushes so they'd dry in the bright sun.

"You seem to like swimming, a lot," I said with a smile. "How was the trip down?" I joked.

"Not too bad," she smiled, "once I swam up from all those frothy bubbles. I don't think I want to do it again. And, just for the record, the last dip in the pond wasn't my fault." Abby was wringing out her buckskin shirt.

"Oh no," she said.

"What?" I asked.

"The amulet. It's gone," she moaned. "Not again!"

"Well, maybe it's in the pool," I offered. We looked at the torrent of water crashing down more than fifty feet from where she fell. Then we looked at each other.

"We can't get in there," I said. "The falling water is too strong and it looks really deep."

"Let's look at the outflow," Abby said and we squished over to the water's exit. Water gushed through a maze of small boulders. The pool looked like an overflowing tea cup. There was no sign of the amulet.

"It could still be deep in that pool," I said. "We could come back later this summer when things dried out. We should be able to find it then."

"I don't think we have much of a choice," Abby sighed. "I hope Grandmother Molly isn't too upset."

"She'll understand," I said. "No one died."

Abby looked at me and shook her head. "I know, it could always be worse. At least we're on the right side of Time and I have the map," she said as she patted the pouch on her hip.

"As long as we really are on the right side of time," I said.

"And if we're not?" Abby said quietly. I looked at her and shook my head.

"Then I'll have to follow orders and stay close to you on the path that leads us home." Abby smiled. We found some dry clothes in the bottom of my pack and baked in the sun while the rest of our clothes dried. Soon we were on our way to Grandmother Molly's village.

....

It was late afternoon when we walked into the clearing. Wisps of smoke from last night's roast beast danced in the air. The blackened spit, eager for its next victim, was stretched out on a nearby table. Two village dogs searching for their breakfast were licking up the cold grease, hoping for any morsel that might be related to food. One of them looked up at the sound of our boots on the leafy path.

"Bear!" Abby shouted. "Here, boy." And Bear came lumbering over to greet us, tail wagging. After the required face-licking and patting, Abby and I headed down the path to Grandmother Molly's with Bear close to our heels.

"Hey, Hiram!" I shouted. He stood at the edge of their garden, hoe in hand doing battle against the dandelions that were beginning to bud. He turned and waved. By the time we got close enough for a conversation, we could see Grandmother Molly standing at the screen door.

"Better come up quick," she said. "The black flies have just hatched and are pretty hungry." I shook Hiram's hand in passing, and Abby gave him a quick hug. In a moment, all four of us were on the screened-in porch. Bear headed under the porch to nap in the cool dirt. The black flies stayed outside. You could see the black clouds of the devil's complaint moving and re-forming, as if a swarm was something that breathed.

After greetings with Grandmother Molly, we got caught up on our trip.

"How long have we been gone?" I asked.

"About two weeks," Hiram said.

"We were there only days," Abby pointed out. "Why is that?"

"It's something only the spirits can tell us, and they've been pretty quiet about it," Grandmother Molly explained. "But you're right, the clock seems to move faster here. Tell us about what happened," she said.

When Abby finished the story of the Stone People and the Nighthawk's demise, Grandmother Molly seemed to be staring at her.

"Did something happen to the amulet?" she asked. "Or have you put it in a safe place?" Grandmother Molly's sharp eyes missed nothing.

Abby dropped her head a bit. "I slipped and went over the waterfall. When I came up on shore, it was gone."

"It is fitting," Grandmother Molly said.

"Fitting how?" I asked.

"The amulet has gone home with Katahdin. He has claimed it back. That waterfall is one door to the spirit world. Do not look for it or you may not return to us." Awasosqua paused.

"You're not angry?" Abby asked her.

"Angry? Not at all. We're only pleased you were able to see my father again. How is he?"

"He's well, and older this time. He seems a little slower. Grey Wolf sends his love to you," Abby related.

"Now that you have the stone, you will still be able to travel there, and by shorter routes. What's wrong?" Grandmother Molly asked.

"Let's take a quick walk. The wind has come up and those devils won't be bothering us," Abby offered. The two left Hiram and me on the porch. Bear had dragged himself out from under and was close on Abby's heels.

"How does it feel not to have the black wings following you, Charlie Bear Claw?" Hiram asked.

"Can't say I miss them much," I said. "But the effect is the same when I think about it perching on the ridge, its coal-red eyes burning holes in my mind. So that's where I am. Sometimes I feel they've melted part of my brain and I would rather see the wings than think about them."

"It sounds to me that you've got some work to do. You know you have to come to terms? And what will happen if you don't?" Hiram pulled out a plug of tobacco from his Prince Albert can and tamped it down into the bowl of his briar pipe. He struck a wooden match on his suspender buckle. Soon the smell of sweet tobacco spread through the cabin.

"I know," I said. "It will always be with me and it'll make me act crazy. That about right?"

"You know, if you had replied seriously, I wouldn't have believed what you said for a second. But a smart answer from you? I know you've got things under control. But if you need to talk, you know how to find me." Hiram pulled on his pipe. "You still haven't found your special spot, as I recall."

Hiram put his pipe down. Somehow the smell of the tobacco reminded me of the smoke ceremony, something that always put me at ease. Being calm was important in finding one's special place.

"I know, I'm still looking," I said. I could see Molly and Abby making their way back from their walk. Knowing what they had been talking about was driving my curiosity, but I had to wait until later. They came in the porch, and sat down.

"We're going to the potlatch for dinner," Grandmother Molly said. "I understand there may be some kind of throwing contest." She looked at Abby and smiled.

"I have no idea what you're talking about," said Abby, who picked up a small stone and knocked a pine cone off a nearby branch.

We finished our tea and took the path to the common ground. Picnic tables were set out, and an elevated stage that doubled as a dance floor poked out from under a rain fly above it. Grandmother Molly brought a chicken casserole. Abby was carrying some fresh gingerbread and the makings of whip cream. It was a great feast. We had a good time, and we felt like we were home.

"See that man by the fire pit?" I asked Abby.

"You mean the one in the tall hat who looks like Gesonka's twin?" she replied.

"That's the one," I said. "Do you know who he is?" I asked her.

"Let's find out," and with that she got up and began to walk over to him. I was right behind her. Another man joined him.

"And that guy looks just like Moulsem," I said on the way over. Gesonka's twin looked up at us.

"Hi, I don't think we've met," Abby said to the one in the tall hat.

"We have not," he replied. "My name is George Francis. And this guy with the red fox tail is Mike Gideon, my cousin from Princeton."

"You're a long way from home," Abby said. "Princeton is way Down East."

"I visit once in a while," Mike said, his red fox tail jiggling behind his head as he spoke.

"That red fox tail," I said, "is something I've seen only once before."

"Where was that?" Mike replied. I was about to answer, when George interrupted.

"It's a family thing," he said. "Legend has it that one of Mike's ancestors, a brave hunter, always hung a red fox tail from his hat." Abby and I looked at each other, thinking of the possibilities. "And I have an ancestor who was supposedly a brother to Mike's."

"That's pretty special," Abby said. "Was he a hunter, too?"

"They were both well known for their hunting skills, but more importantly they protected their tribe from those who would destroy it," George said. We chatted a minute more and then excused ourselves for more food. I had a lot of eating to catch up on. The diet at Grey Wolf's wasn't quite what I was used to.

"Can you believe it?" Abby asked. "We actually hung out with their fabled ancestors?"

"I know," I said. "I can't seem to get my head wrapped around it." We walked toward the dance stage.

"You know what happens when we all work together?" I asked her after the dance music started and we had joined other couples on the stage.

"What?" She asked.

"Good things," I whispered. "Good things." And she tightened her hands.

....

The next morning the sun beat into the bunkhouse. It might have been close to five, and I could feel the heat coming on early. The recent high humidity left us begging for a cold front to push T-showers our way and cool things down to normal. Abby was waking up.

I leaned over. "Want to tell me about Erik?" I asked. "Or aren't you awake enough."

She groaned. From under the covers her reply suggested the latter. I got up and fired up the Coleman grill. In ten minutes, we'd have hot coffee. A quick trip to the outside shower, and I was ready for the last leg of our trip back to the Katahdin Inn. I looked over at the bed. Abby hadn't moved an inch. The sheet fluttered with every breath. I grabbed my coffee and walked out to the woodpile.

The chopping block made a great seat with a view through the trees right above the sharply descending rapids we called Grand Pitch. I felt a kind of peace I hadn't known since I was little. It wasn't long before Hiram stepped out of the tree line and walked over, his pipe sweetening the morning air.

"Hey, Charlie," he said as he sat on a bench used for splitting cedar shakes. "Have you been looking for your spot?"

"Sometimes I think I'll never find it, but this morning it feels pretty nice to be sitting here on this chopping block, listening to the Winter Wren serenade me," I explained. "The sound of the wind in that big pine is pretty nice, too."

"Some days that's all you can hope for," Hiram offered. "Awasosqua told me that Abby learned about Erik the Red."

"Abby hasn't said," I replied.

"Well, when and if she does, just know that nothing bad happened back then," Hiram said.

"I know a red-haired boy named Erik," I said. "Olive's nephew or something like that."

"From the old village at the end of Gero?" Hiram asked.

"I think so," I said. "He mentioned that his parents died in a boat accident, but I hadn't heard of one. Have you?"

Hiram thought a minute. "No, I haven't. You might ask Cookee at the Dam. He'd know, keeps his ear to the phone all day, I wager."

"We're heading home after breakfast," I said.

"Have you been thinking about black wings?" he asked.

"A little," I replied. "I'm still pretty angry about how they've tormented me."

"Acceptance isn't always easy. It's like dealing with Caleb. You always know he'll stand for himself over anyone else." Hiram knocked out the ashes from his pipe.

"I keep wondering if they'll show up again," I said. "And then I get a little crazy."

"South Wind crazy?" Hiram asked. He filled his pipe. Bear wandered over, caging for a treat.

"Yep, that bad," I replied, as I dig into my pocket and produced some dog-quality deer jerky. Bear was careful not to nip my finger-tips when he ripped it away from my hand.

"If you recognize it coming on, you can stop it, too," Hiram suggested.

"It's not that easy," I said. "But I'm getting better at it." We talked a bit about the adventures Abby and I just had.

"I'm heading up the lake soon after you go," he said. "I have to take care of a few things around the camp, but I plan to come back in a few days. Well, we'll see you for breakfast soon?"

"As soon as sleepy head gets vertical," I replied, nodding toward the bunkhouse. "Shouldn't be too long now." Hiram got up, scratched Bear behind the ears, and disappeared back into the trees. My mind was filled with scenes of black wings cruising the tree-tops, coal-red eyes burning into my mind, and the sudden *whoosh* of air flowing between feathers just overhead. It was going to take a while for the patina of Time to make those seem less of a threat.

Abby finally got herself together. She was really anxious about the missing amulet. We packed up and headed to Grandmother Molly's for some breakfast.

After breakfast, Grandmother Molly and Hiram walked us to the carry that led to the top of Grand Pitch. We loaded up our canoe, and as we were about to push off, I called for Bear. He joined us, black fur dripping wet from an earlier swim when he thought he could catch a red squirrel scooting across the eddy. Pointing the bow into the current and at a slight angle, we ferried to the other side with no problem. After we made it into the take-out eddy there, we put the canoe away, waved a final goodbye to Grandmother Molly and Hiram, and walked up to the new road we could see from shore. Wangan and other traffic there would give us many opportunities for a ride back to the Dam.

But it wasn't a wangan we first saw passing by. Heading away from the Dam, Louis drove by in one of our delivery trucks followed by Uncle Amos and Father riding shotgun right behind. Louis braked hard, causing Uncle Amos to tag his rear bumper in the cloud of golden dust.

"Damn it, Louis, what the hell are you trying to do, get us all killed?" came Father's voice from the settling dust. Louis smiled.

"How do I even put up with this abuse?" Louis asked me. "Want a ride? We're going to town to check out the new factory." At this point, Father had gotten out and walked around the back of the truck toward us.

"You're just in time," Father said beating the dust off his cap. "We're on our way to Dover to check out our new business."

"A factory?" I asked him.

"Not just any factory," Father replied. "It's a real money-maker!"

"What?" I asked.

"Never mind, just hop in and you'll see." Bear and I jumped onto the truck bed with our gear, and Abby hopped inside the cab with Louis who gave us the newest details of the King family alcohol business.

Back to Business
Chapter 17

"We should not be doing that," I said loudly, slamming the flat of my hand on the table. The sudden wind blew a chair off the porch. Father looked so startled I thought he had just laid a goose egg. Louis jumped about a foot, but Uncle Amos didn't bat an eyelash. Abby was squeezing my arm. Bear scurried off after something that was moving in a nearby pile of brush.

"Charlie?" Amos said. "Try to relax." The wind died a little, then was gone.

We were gathered on the front porch of the biggest distillery in Maine. It was all legal, even in Prohibition, especially in Prohibition. Folks had to have their medicinal alcohol and doctors were too ready to write the scripts needed. Such alcohol was produced and semi-carefully audited. And in spite of that protocol, both Katahdin Special and *Tanglefoot* were made there. In the King's newest business move, the family bought the licensed, commercial distillery. No one seemed to care who the family was. No one came knocking to see. On top of all of that, the government helped us pay for it with some silly grant money.

I continued my rant. "Don't you see what Martin is up to?"

"He's a good customer," Father said. "And his money will be difficult to replace."

"You should listen to Charlie," Uncle Amos said. "He's had people looking."

"What? Looking at what?" Caleb exploded.

"Martin re-sells to Boston at close to cost. His one percent is still a lot of money due to the sheer volume," Amos explained. "Listen to him, Caleb.”

“We stop selling to Martin. His customers will come to us directly and we can charge them more for the privilege of dealing with us in person,” I said. I didn’t take my eyes off Father. It was a staring contest that I was determined not to lose. “It won’t take long. Besides, we now have the plant and plenty of cash is coming in legally.”

“Kinda takes all the fun out of it,” Louis remarked. Abby and Amos laughed. Even Father smiled a little.

“As long as this ‘fun’ doesn’t become bodily harm or worse.” The laughter stopped as if I had hit a switch. “You think the Boston Gang is wanting to pay more? I doubt that. We need to prepare for trouble in case they suddenly expect a discount on having Martin gone.”

“But what can we do?” Abby asked.

“We can hire extra men at the plant,” I said. “I think Father can find someone for night watchman around the Inn.”

“I got a guy who’ll call us from the Dam if anyone suspicious shows up,” Amos said. “And there’s one at the tramway on the Carry upriver.”

“As long as they don’t cut the line,” Caleb said. “It has happened before.” He looked down, seemingly ashamed of having been caught. It was a good act nonetheless. He almost had me fooled, but the man has a ‘tell.’ He drops his head when he wants you to believe him. He wasn’t ashamed at all.

“Alright, back to the matter at hand,” I said. “We have to agree that there won’t be any side deals, that means none at all. Does everyone understand that?” Amos, Louis and Father nodded their heads.

“You get that, Louis?” I asked.

“I do. I won’t sell to Mickey anymore,” he answered. Mickey was one of the cops we had been bribing since the beginning.

“How about you, Uncle Amos? Any side deals you’ll be missing?” I asked him. He cocked his head.

“Just the one with the lawyer we hired,” he replied.

“Maybe you ought to keep that one,” I said.

“Don’t mind if I do,” Amos replied.

“And you, Father? You’re the one that can make or break us. You have to give up the deals with Martin and anyone else.”

Father sighed, but he looked right at me and said, “I can give them up. The new plant will be keeping me busy. I’m going to have to move down here to manage it. So, I won’t have time for side deals. Besides, I’ll be getting a regular paycheck every Friday.” He smiled.

Finally, I thought, Father can actually be a member of a team.

Once we all agreed what was made where, the rest was easy. The barrels were filled and shipped from our village like usual. Cases came from the re-processing plant clearly marked "Medicinal." The Revenooers weren't looking too hard when cases of *Tanglefoot* got unloaded in back of Mike's speakeasy off Oyster Street in Beantown. If there's a thirst, there's something for it.

We unloaded the cases of moonshine for distribution later on, and headed back to the Dam without Father. He was staying to manage everything, although there was a lady, so-to-speak, who boarded at the Dover House where he was staying.

In light of what happened next, none of this was a great idea.

Louis and Uncle Amos were in one truck. Abby and I in the other. We had been eating dust for miles since we drove up Blair Hill in Greenville. We had been quiet for a while. I was thinking about catching trout in Bear Stream Pond we had just driven by, when Abby brought me back to the dusty cab.

"You were pretty insistent earlier, Charlie. It didn't seem like you were yourself," Abby said. "Care to comment?"

"I've had enough," I replied. "I realized I had to be that way to get the others to listen to me."

"Do you realize how much you sounded like Caleb?" she observed. "I hope that won't be permanent."

"Don't worry," I said. "I'm aware and it's not. I don't like responding that way. The last thing I want is to become my father." We let that hang in the air until we pulled into the Chesuncook Dam Road.

It was dark when we pulled into the Dam a mile later. Kerosene lights from the sitting room cast golden drapes over the porch and the narrow steps leading up to it. This time we had crowded into the cab with me riding shotgun and Abby on my lap. As soon as the wheels stopped moving, but probably a second or two before, the doors flew open, we piled out, the truck jerked to a stop, engine dead, in that order. Louis and Uncle Amos were just ahead of us, pulled off into the little parking area beside the barn.

"Guess that's one way to park it," Louis said walking over. The truck was angled with the front half nearly in the ditch. "Think we can get something to eat from Cookee?"

"Let's ask," said Uncle Amos, holding a paper sack. "I've got a little delivery for him. And no, this is not a side deal," he said, and smiled. We followed him up to the porch and waited outside where two river drivers were playing checkers.

"You can't do that," we heard one of them say. That was quickly followed by, "Oh I certainly can. The directions are printed right here." That figure was just around the corner of the wraparound porch and out of sight. I didn't know if a gun or knife were 'the directions,' or if he really was going to read something when I heard him say, "When the opposing side…." Then I relaxed. Uncle Amos appeared on the other side of the screen door and motioned us inside. We stepped into the outer parlor. Two men were reading and a third was heading up the stairs, treads covered with tiny pin pricks from many pair of caulked boots. We hung up our stuff and walked into the long dining room, taking seats along one end of a table that must have sat twenty or more.

"They're coming," Uncle Amos said quietly when we were finishing up our meal. The pot roast was served with carrots and potatoes, one of the better ones here. Fitting for a last supper, I thought.

"That didn't take long," Louis said. "What did he do, call 'em up and tell 'em the minute we left?"

"Probably something like that. You know how much he thinks of himself," Uncle Amos said.

"Shouldn't we be heading up the lake right now?" I asked.

"Not unless you want to swim part of the way home," Louis said. "The search light burned out weeks ago. Heading out with no searchlight, no moonlight, no starlight, whitecaps everywhere, and what's that other nagging little thing? 'Pulpwood?' you ask? You'll never see the one that you drive through the hull until it rests in your lap."

"Alright, take it easy Louis," Uncle Amos said. "They were seen getting off the Boston Express at the Junction. I expect they'll be on their way across Moosehead at first light."

"That'll put them at the Boom House at five or six tomorrow," I said. "We can leave at first light and be ready for them well before they arrive."

"If the boat starts," Uncle Amos said. "I'll tell Caleb. He'll need to keep a sharp eye for the next few days." Uncle Amos headed to a little cabin he used when he had to stay over. Louis trekked upstairs to the ram pasture, and Abby and I climbed the ladder in the barn to sleep in the loft.

We spread out the bottom blanket and were soon covered with a comfy horse quilt. "Remember Erik with the red hair? Olive's nephew?" I asked.

"He's been in my thoughts lately," Abby replied.

"I can't imagine why," I said, fishing.

"We both have red hair. So what?" Abby challenged.

"I was just wondering if you were wondering, that's all," I said.

"Thanks for caring, Charlie. Sorry if I seemed a little defensive. I don't know what to make of any of it."

"We don't have a plan," I said, changing the subject.

"I know. There doesn't seem to be one," she observed.

"I think some rock throwing should be involved," I said.

"I think I know someone who could make you happy with that skill," Abby quipped and rolled over facing me.

"Let's be serious." We stopped laughing at the same time. "We don't have a plan," I said.

"You already said that," she muttered.

"I would like to point out that I still mean it, as much as I did a minute ago," I said.

"What do you think the Boston Gang intends to do?" Abby asked.

"Kill us and burn us out. Pretty straightforward, wouldn't you say?" I asked.

"I'd say. Guess we should do something about that. While Uncle Amos and Louis polish up their rifles, I have a non-violent plan to share. But you can't say it came from me, or the men won't listen." And Abby told me her plan.

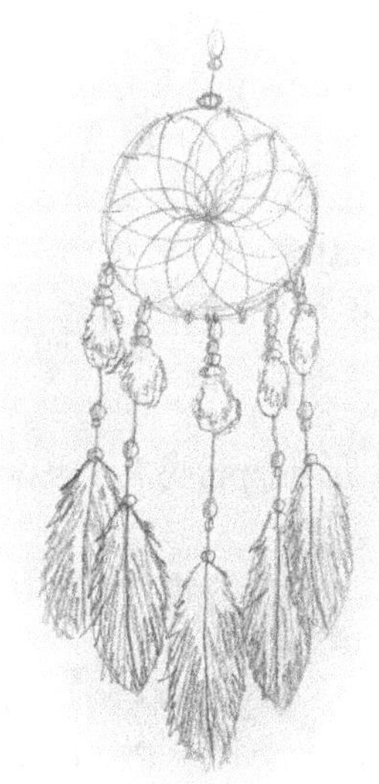

Paths
Chapter 18

The next morning, we finished breakfast by 4:30 right after the river drivers, and had *The Twilight* purring quietly as it warmed up, exhaust burbling as a slight swell gave us a carnival ride trying to walk the plank-way. Just as soon as we could see what was in the water in front of us, Louis threw the last line, leaving it on the dock. Uncle Amos backed her out into the dark grey lake, threw the brass lever forward and gave her all the gas she could take. It was a fast trip with a strong south wind and we tagged just one small piece of driftwood that took a chip out of a high clapboard. A rag fixed that pretty quick. We tied up at the Village dock, and ran for the Katahdin Inn. Bear nosed us to the door but took a sharp turn to chase after the fish Blind Bill had just heaved up from his dock down below the lake's edge. He chased that shiny chub across the lawn not seeming to know just what to do with it. Olive was in the kitchen.

"Just in time," she smiled at us. "Muffins just coming out. So glad you're back."

"I'm starving," I said.

"You just ate," Abby remarked. "Not two hours ago."

"It took a lot of energy to get us up the lake so fast," I tried to explain. Time was not our friend in this case. I summoned Sowanakik to push us home, and that effort was exhausting.

"What's going on?" Olive asked, eyebrows raised as she pulled out two long tins of golden-brown muffins, sugar glistening on their tops. Abby explained what was going on.

"It's just for a day or so," Abby finished. She looked around.

"Where's Erik?" she asked.

"He went across the lake to help out at my sister's not long after you left, Olive explained." We decided that was a safe thing to do. Louis would take Olive and Bear over after lunch. We called the depot there to let her know that she was coming to visit for a few days.

We moved into the parlor, muffins in hand. My hand, that is. Louis and Uncle Amos held steaming coffee mugs.

"What are we going to do?" Abby asked.

"We're going to meet them up river with a surprise," I said between muffin bites.

"The only surprise they need is some buckshot between the cheeks. Takes a long while to pick the shot out," Louis said.

"We set up at the carry after the last cart for the day has crossed. They'll walk the carry with their gear to a canoe they probably swapped out for." I explained. They're in a hurry. Losing Martin must really hurt their bottom line. I brushed crumbs off my shirt.

"And we ambush them! Brilliant idea," Louis remarked, burnishing his shot-gun's barrel with an oiled cloth.

"No, not quite like that," I sighed. "We want to make them an offer."

"A what?" Uncle Amos chimed in.

"I set up two man-traps. They swing from the birch by their feet until we cut them down," I explain. I'd seen Moosis and the hunters do the same thing trapping game.

"Taking them alive means that we have direct messengers. That's leverage. We keep them safe in the plant for the time being," I reasoned. "I can take care of the rest."

"I don't get why I can't just shoot 'em," Louis mourned as if he had just missed the biggest buck in the forest. "You're asking for trouble if you let them live."

"And that's what we'll get plenty of if we continue a war we don't need!" My anger was bringing up the wind again. It didn't last long. I was exhausted at the thought of sustaining it. At times like this, I really, really wanted to be sitting on the maple chopping block outside Grandmother Molly's woodshed.

"Okay, Charlie, you can relax. We won't kill them." Louis said. And in a lower voice, "as much as I think we should." I stared at Louis. I couldn't deal with much more of him.

"Then we have a plan," I said. "I'm going to call Father at the plant to let him know he'll be having company for dinner."

"Louis, you get the ropes we'll need," Uncle Amos said. "We'll boat up river. I heard the men at the Dam say they were going to let some water out to flush pulp down from Little Ragamuff, so we can make it all the way up to the Carry just as soon as Louis gets back from taking Olive and Bear over to Gero."

"Remember, Charlie? Our pulpwood surprise?" Abby reminded me. I could still see her stranded on a pile of wood in the middle of the rapids like it happened this morning.

"Let's not let that happen again," I answered. It wasn't long before Louis returned. He cut the outboard and coasted in alongside the float.

We piled into the bateau, the ropes coiled at our feet, and a couple of rifles in case things didn't work out as planned. A couple of hours later, we had set up camp across from the Carry entrance and were on our way to set up the traps.

Looking back on things, it went smooth as silk. They walked right into trouble, and found themselves hoisted in the air by their legs. We cut down the two surprised men one at a time, tied their hands, got them in the bateau and headed back. The two would-be assassins were cowering in the bateau, shivering from the cold, late afternoon air. After a couple of hours, we pulled over by an old, unused dock to make some lunch.

"You're gonna be sorry," the shorter one said.

"And why might that be so?" I replied.

"Because the boss is my father," he replied with a smile.

"Good to know," I said. "My father would love to meet you both." Now I knew my plan would work.

It took some persuading before Uncle Amos and Louis were on board with what Abby and I proposed. After I explained that we had learned a different trail but needed to tie the men together with us so they couldn't escape, Louis and Uncle Amos went back downriver in the bateau. Abby took us on a spirit path. When it led by two ancient villages, we were tempted to drop these two off and be done with them, but they were useful and we didn't want to upset the timestream. About ten minutes later, the four of us popped out of the woods in a small clearing behind Father's plant. We marched them into the opening of an unused loading dock and tied the surplus rope around a full barrel of heavy gear oil just outside the door. They weren't going anywhere wearing blindfolds and their hands tied behind their backs.

Abby kept watch while I found Father in his office staring out the large windows. We could see the opening of the loading dock and one of our prisoners. Father was reaching for his black cloak hanging from the tree by his desk.

"It looks like they're all tied up," Father said. He swung his cloak over his shoulders. The sun must have been in just the right spot, as all I could see was a pair of black wings. I must have looked startled. I was.

"Hey, are you okay?" I heard him ask.

The image took a moment to clear. "I think so. The sun seemed to blind me for a moment." I rubbed my eyes, not entirely sure of what I had just seen. "They're not going anywhere," I said. "I checked the ropes and Abby's keeping an eye on them."

"What's next?" Father asked.

"Get in touch with Boston. We need to let them know that we'll keep the son until they can assure us they will stop interfering in our business. Let the tall one take the message back with him. When Boston agrees, we'll release the son."

"It's a good plan," Father said. "I hope they'll keep their word."

Soon, we were ready to cut the tall one loose. Father paid for his train ticket. When the response came back, our second guest was on his way and the war was averted for now.

"We can take a path home, right?" I asked.

"We can," Abby said, "but know what might be more fun? Taking a path to where we can see dinosaurs."

"I don't think I want to see any of those unless they're in a book," I answered. It was good to be going home. At least I'll have found my special place beside Grandmother Molly's woodshed.

Abby led us home from the distillery. It was good to know there was a strong demand for medicinal alcohol. Charlatans like Dr. Kilmer used our alcohol for his "Snake Root Elixir." It made him a millionaire. We were going to do better than he did.

Our path ended in the field in front of the Village church and schoolhouse, and in the right timestream, too. Abby and I made our way to the Katahdin View Inn. Bear ran out to greet us, nearly knocking us onto the ground. We bumped into Erik coming around the corner.

"What's the hurry?" Abby asked with a smile as we stepped aside.

"Aunt Olive has to have more eggs right away," he said, scampering for the hen house.

"Good to know some things haven't changed," I observed. "I

really wonder about that red hair.”

“And his name, too,” said Abby. “He’s probably a distant relative, maybe a cousin or something. Wish I could ask Dad.” Abby held something in her hand. I could see it was a small gold cross and chain. “It was his,” she said. “He got it from the Bible salesman just before we went up river to bring down the logs.” A tear fell down her cheek. She sighed and folded the little cross back into her pocket.

“I wish we could ask him, too,” I said. “But we’re here. No more Nighthawk. No spirits contacting us over the centuries.”

“Let’s hope so,” she said. “As long as there wasn’t a second nest we missed.”

Hand in hand, we walked to the Katahdin View Lodge to help Olive feed the woodcutters who had just stepped off the boat. Most had no idea what waited for them in the camps, just as I had no idea if we’d continue to evade the revenooers. At least I knew I wouldn’t be seeing any black wings, and that was good enough. Or so I hoped.

Annotated Bibliography

Bruchak, *Thirteen Moons on Turtle's Back, The Winter People, Night Wings, The Hunter's Promise*

Cook, *Above the Gravel Bar, The Native canoe routes of Mane*

Ekstrom, Fanny Hardy; *The Penobscot Man*

Glaster, Charles; *The West Brancher*
> Glaster was in charge of converting from tree length to 4 foot pulp about 1915. He was at the West Branch boom house where, at 5PM, he received the call about Alec Gunn's boat on fire in the thoroughfare behind Gero Island November 22, 1920. Good, general information about logging in the Maine woods during the pandemic.

Pike, Richard, *Tall Trees and Tough Men*

Smith, Marion Whitney;
> Pamphlets published by the Millinocket Historical Museum include Abenaki myths

About the Author

Brad Edwards writes in a small cabin on the shore of Chesuncook Lake within the old Village. Life in the Village of 1920 is not much different today from that described within the pages of this series. The lake was the primary "road" for supplies with Alec Gunn's *Hunky Dory* (*The Twilight*) bringing people, fuel and supplies eighteen miles from the Dam to the Village. When the water is low, Edwards can be seen scoping out drowned piers, cast off engines, and final resting places of *The A.B. Smith* and the *John Ross* as he reads tales of the Wabanaki written by Joseph Bruchac.